PRAISE FOR THE TENSORATE SERIES

"Joyously wild stuff. Highly recommended."

—**N. K. Jemisin,** *The New York Times*

"Yang conjures up a world of magic and machines, wild monsters and sophisticated civilizations, that you'll want to return to again and again."

—**Annalee Newitz,** *Ars Technica*

"Full of love and loss, confrontation and discovery. Each moment is a glistening pearl, all strung together in a wonder of world-creation."

—**Ken Liu, Nebula, Hugo, and World Fantasy Award winner and author of** *The Grace of Kings* **and** *The Paper Menagerie*

"I love JY Yang's effortlessly fascinating world-building."

—**Kate Elliott, author of** *Black Wolves* **and** *Court of Fives*

"A fascinating world of battles, politics, magic, and romance."

—Zen Cho, author of Sorcerer to the Crown

"Filled with memorable characters and set in a wonderfully imaginative and original universe."

—**Aliette de Bodard, Nebula Award–winning author of** *The House of Shattered Wings*

"Like a Miyazaki movie decided to jump off the screen and sear itself into prose, and in doing so became something entirely new."

—**Indrapramit Das, author of** *The Devourers*

"Relentlessly captivating, heartbreaking, and powerful."

—**Fran Wilde, award-winning, Nebula and Hugo–nominated author of** *Updraft, Cloudbound,* **and** *Horizon*

"Yang's prose carries the reader along. . . . A really good book."

—*Locus*

"Yang deftly creates a world infused with magic, story, and hierarchy."

—**Joel Cunningham,** *B&N Sci-Fi and Fantasy Blog*

"Yang captures an epic sweep in compact, precise prose."

—*Publishers Weekly* **(starred review)**

ALSO BY JY YANG

The Tensorate Series

The Black Tides of Heaven
The Red Threads of Fortune

JY YANG

THE DESCENT OF MONSTERS

A TOM DOHERTY ASSOCIATES BOOK

NEW YORK

THE DESCENT OF MONSTERS

Copyright © 2018 by JY Yang

Cover illustration by Yuko Shimizu
Cover design by Christine Foltzer

Map by Serena Maylon

Edited by Carl Engle-Laird

A Tor.com Book
Published by Tom Doherty Associates
175 Fifth Avenue
New York, NY 10010

www.tor.com

Tor® is a registered trademark of
Macmillan Publishing Group, LLC.

ISBN 978-1-250-16585-5 (trade paperback)
ISBN 978-1-250-16584-8 (ebook)

First Edition: July 2018

To my gang of blowholes, you know who you are.

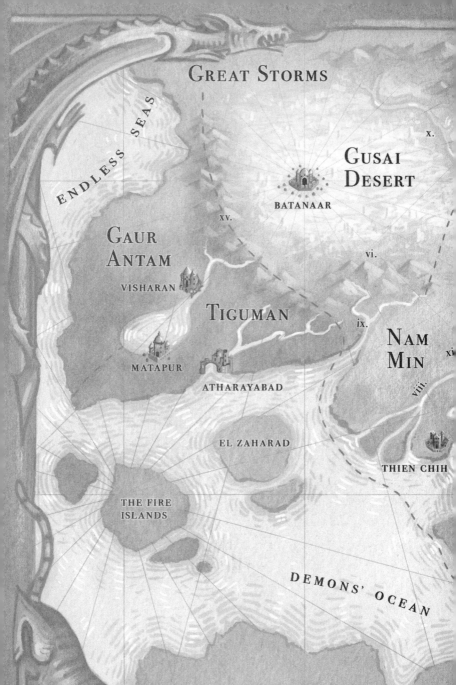

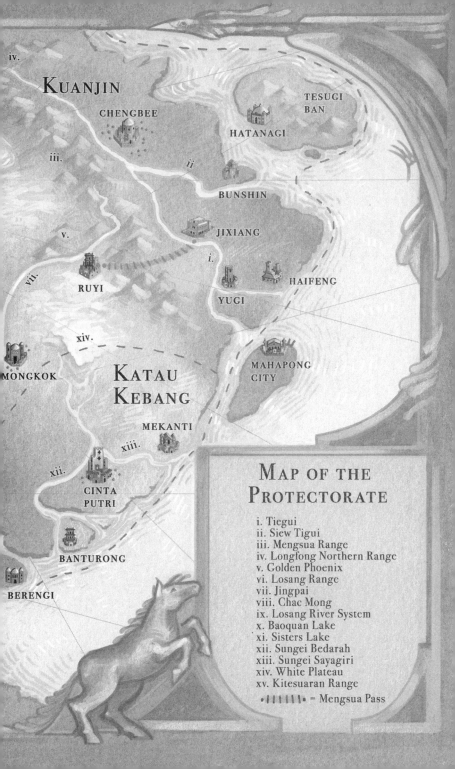

Prologue

My beloved twin:

It is strange, writing a letter to someone you may never meet. Twenty-six years ago we were separated on the shores of the Demons' Ocean, too young to do anything but breathe and suckle and cry. Our lives diverged: you taken to the deepest interior of the Protectorate, cocooned in secrecy at the heart of one of the empire's biggest lies, and I exiled to the fringes of society, never quite belonging anywhere.

I spent my life in ignorance of your existence, convinced that there was no other like me. And then I learned the truth from the woman who attended our birth all those years ago, the handmaiden who witnessed the sale of two helpless infants and carried that secret as a weight in her heart for decades. Suddenly I understood why I had always felt there was some part of me missing.

But no more. I have spent the past two years searching for you as the Protectorate slowly spiraled toward civil war. I found where they kept you. And now my quest to rescue you begins. I have never done anything more dangerous. If I succeed, you will never have to read this letter, because I will tell you all of this firsthand. This letter, really, is for myself to read in the long days ahead. It is a record, and it is a promise.

I will find you. I will not give up.

Your twin,
Rider

PART ONE

THE INVESTIGATOR

To My Beloved Kayan

Kayan, my sweet flower:

You're reading this because I'm dead. That's right, I'm doing that thing you hate in the weeklies you read, writing a last letter to my beloved because I expect to die. And my expectations have been excruciatingly accurate of late, so I'll be surprised if I have to trash this. Surprised, and embarrassed.

But don't worry—death circling overhead hasn't turned me into a sentimental fool. This is not some misbegotten love letter or ode to a life unlived. As if I'd write that kind of horseshit.

Fuck that. This is a call to arms. This isn't me feeling sorry for myself. I am burning with fury at the injustice I have encountered.

You were right, Kayan. You said that this job would kill me someday, and it has. Your prize is losing the only person who's ever meant anything to you. Congratulations.

You remember my last letter to you? The one

where I told you about the mountain disaster case I'd been given? Remember I said it smelled rotten? It was. That case went sour, real fast. The fruit was putrid to the core. <u>Some</u> news must filter out to your boat even on the unforgiving slush of the Demons' Ocean, so you might have heard that the investigation closed recently, with all the blame pushed to the Machinists. Of course that shit isn't true. The report carried my name, but neither my approval nor my complicity. Well, fuck. I guess it had my complicity. But I signed off on that heap of stinking lies to get them off my back. Since then I've been chasing the truth across the slimy under-belly of the Protectorate because the fortunes will cut off my tongue and hands before I let this stand unchallenged.

Well my love, it's been days of wading deeper and deeper into foaming sewage. There's a madness at the bottom of all this and I fear I haven't even looked it in the face. The shit that's gone down here is stranger than I could have ever imagined.

No doubt the Protectorate will spend the next few days smearing me as a traitor, a barbarian, a Kebangilan reprobate who couldn't help but revert to her uncivilized nature despite her Kuanjin up-bringing. All their usual nonsense—we know how they work, don't we? I've worked for them for a dozen years, after all.

But you, my love—<u>you</u> will know the truth. Look. Here are the compiled journals, notes, and memos I've stacked up over the past few weeks. I suspected all along—hell, I <u>knew</u>—that it was all going to end in flames. Read these things. Read them, and understand what I'm sacrificing myself for. Read them, and then get fucking livid, like I did. Follow this gravesent affair to its bitter end. Anything else would be rank injustice, and I know how you feel about that. I trust you.

I know you're going to make them <u>pay</u>.

Your beloved,
Sariman

Chapter One

PREPARED BY TENSOR CHUWAN SARIMAN

Here begins the preliminary report into the so-called Rewar Teng Incident, compiled by Tensor Chuwan Sariman. On this fourteenth day of the seventh month of the year 1162, I declare the investigation into the aforementioned incident open. By the grace of the Protector and the powers invested in me by the Ministry of Justice, I will lead the investigation into what happened on that terrible day. Where there was a jungle of fear and uncertainty, there shall be the shape of hidden things revealed. Where there were storms of lies, there will be truth. No expense shall be spared, no question left unanswered. The special investigation I lead will be relentless in the pursuit of justice, and whatever obstacles are determined to come my way should take heed, for I shall be merciless. No ocean, nor mountain, nor burning fire shall deter me. My will is absolute and my mandate clear. I will not rest until the reality of what happened is laid bare. And all my efforts shall not go to waste, for through understanding the tapestry of circumstances that led to this tragedy, we shall prevent it from ever happening again.

THE INCIDENT

On the fourth day of the seventh month, it was registered with Senior Tensor Chu Xinyang of the Academy that the Rewar Teng Institute of Experimental Methods had failed to send in their weekly report and list of supply orders, as they had been due to. Further investigation revealed that family and acquaintances of institute staff had not been able to contact them for the past five days, although that had been attributed to ill weather, as the monsoons had destroyed a relay tower in the Mengsua Pass and disrupted land communications. But the storms passed, and still the silence persisted. On the sixth day of the seventh month, Tensor Chu dispatched a team northward to make contact with the institute and find out what happened.

Upon arrival at the institute, the special group found

waiting for them a scene of disaster. The premises were a sea of blood and bones, and of the forty-two Tensors who had been registered to work at the Institute, there was no other sign. A swift and thorough investigation of the site drew a clear and unfortunate conclusion. All the residents of the Institute had been killed, both human and animal, and furthermore, it had been one of the Institute's experiments that was responsible for the massacre.

The culprit was determined to be one of the large raptor-naga crossbreeds, whose carcass was discovered in the caverns beneath the Institute. Unlike the other bodies on the premises, the crossbreed was found freshly slain, the blood still liquid. With an abundance of wisdom, Tensor Yesai, who had been leading the team, determined that either survivors remained of the Institute's staff, or that there were interlopers on the premises.

An armed search was immediately carried out, and the team discovered two outlaws hiding within the caverns, the Machinist terrorist leader Sanao Akeha and a female companion whose identity has yet to be determined. They were swiftly apprehended and taken into custody, and the institute secured.

Teams are on site to recover and process evidence that will unlock the truth of the incident. All forty-two residents of the institute are presumed deceased, pending identification of their remains. (Tensor Yesai's overall report can be read appended to this document.)

THE HISTORY OF THE INSTITUTE

The Rewar Teng Institute of Experimental Methods was founded by Tensor M in 1148. Originally called the Rewar Teng Breeding Laboratory, it began operation under the authority of the Institute of Agricultural Development, with a personnel strength of eight. The site, high in the Longfong mountain range, was chosen due to its proximity to the Rewar Teng Slack anomaly, which produced deformations in the Slack useful to experimental procedures. In its early days, the laboratory focused on modifying large southern species to be more resistant to heavier gravity in the north. As a result of its successes, the laboratory was expanded to a personnel strength of twenty-five in 1152, and registered as a separate institute under the auspices of Tensor Sanao Sonami, who was then Agricultural Minister. Additional holding pens and animal handling facilities were built, and the compound was extended to include two new buildings and a dormitory. Tensor M retired in 1157, at which time Tensor R was nominated to head the institute by the Minister.

THE SCOPE OF THE CURRENT INVESTIGATION, AND PROPOSED METHODS

Our knowledge of what happened that day lies in tatters, incomplete and fraying. In order to stitch them back into whole cloth, the investigation must find the answer to these questions:

How did the crossbreed escape its bonds? Was it through caprice or malice that it was loosed upon the institute?

What safeguards did the institute have against such an eventuality? How were these safeguards breached? Did procedural lapses play a part? Or were the safeguards simply inadequate?

How were the outlaws involved in this incident? Can their presence at the site after the disaster be mere coincidence?

Why did five days pass before the extent of the disaster was made known? What protocols can we put in place to ensure a more timely response?

How can we prevent the same from happening again?

Chapter Two

APPENDIX 2

ACCOUNT OF THE STATE OF THE REWAR TENG INSTITUTE UPON ARRIVAL

PREPARED BY TENSOR YESAI

We arrived at the compound just after first sunrise, following the path prescribed to us. The trail upward had been recently cleared, with rockfall debris lining the sides, although there was a layer of fallen leaves on the paving stone. I took this to mean that staff from the institute had cleared the path after the storms but not in the days after. The fence generators around the compound also had not been charged in a few days, and most had run out of power by the time we arrived. Taken together, these observations pointed to the fact that the incident must have happened almost immediately after the storm passed, which is to say about six days ago.

We found the institute devoid of life, animal or human. Entering the courtyard, we came across a good number of bones and partial bodies in states of heavy decomposition, all bearing marks of predation. Our initial assessment estimated at least fourteen human bodies and an unknown number of animal carcasses, presumed to be the remains of the experimental subjects being bred by the institute. The forensics expert, Dr. Inan, determined that the oldest remains were at least a week old, including the bodies which were recognizably human. He also said that the most recent corpses were at least three days old. Most of the bodies had been killed at another location and brought to the courtyard, indicating that the creature treated it as a lair of some kind. At this time, we did not know if the entity responsible for the kills was still in the area, and proceeded as though we were in hostile territory.

We split up into three groups of four. Tensor Ma Feng led the group assigned to examine the administrative building and the power plants, Tensor Quah led the group assigned to examine the dormitories and kitchens, and I led the last group, to examine the laboratory buildings and animal holding pens.

The dormitory group found six more bodies on the second floor, also badly decomposed, and presumed to have died at the same time as did the oldest bodies in the courtyard. Unlike those, these bodies appeared intact, aside from the injuries that were presumably the cause of death. The wound patterns suggested that the six were killed by a smaller beast, quite possibly a domestic raptor, as such creatures were a major component of the laboratory's breeding program. It appeared that the victims had sought shelter on the second floor, barricading the stairway with furniture, a measure which proved ineffective.

A quick search of the dormitory found most of the staff's personal belongings untouched, including clothes, books, toiletries, and keepsakes. These items were later collected by the team; they will be returned to the families of the victims pending completion of the full investigation.

The door to the main laboratory building was found badly damaged; we guessed that this was how the beast entered the facilities. We found evidence that the attack began while work was ongoing. Apparatus had been turned over and smashed, and chemicals left uncovered, some of which had evaporated. From the blood trails, we surmised that the beast had killed the Tensors working there, then dragged them outside at its leisure. The carcasses of two raptors in separate holding pens were presumed to have died from dehydration or starvation in the week after the incident. We recovered a number of laboratory journals from the scene, which will also be handed over to the investigative team as evidence.

The laboratory building had a large annex consisting of a single circular room at least three stories high. There we found the first concrete evidence of the beast that had ravaged the place. The annex was designed to hold at least two megafauna specimens, and from the destruction of the support beams and chains within the room, it was clear that one of those beasts had broken its bonds. The carcass of the other remained in the annex, still chained, and in an advanced state of decay. As far as we could tell—and inasmuch as our guesses were corroborated by what was written in the scientists' notes—the creatures were successful crosses between raptors and nagas. In phenotype, the carcass resembled the former more than the latter, except for its extraordinary size. In other respects, the body was far too decayed for us to draw sufficient conclusions. One of the team noted that it was fascinating how the escaped crossbreed did not turn to the body of its fellow for sustenance, despite it being such a rich source. I concurred.

Behind these buildings we found the animal holding pens. There were five rows of pens, the gates to three of which had been sprung. We assumed that a member of the staff had loosed the animals in hopes of slowing down or stopping the crossbreed. The crossbreed had later torn the gates off the fourth row and presumably killed and consumed the animals kept within, but the fifth row remained intact. The power to the buildings must have failed after a few days, and none of the animals had survived the nights without heating. Light captures of the carcasses are appended to this report.

It was the final team, led by Tensor Ma Feng, that found the most important pieces of evidence. The main administrative buildings are built on top of a fissure that leads to the caverns underground, the source of the Rewar Teng anomaly.

It was in the last of these caverns, however, that we discovered the carcass of the beast. It was an albino creature, and lean but not malnourished. Alive, it must have stood ten yields high and weighed nearly a ton. It had been grievously wounded in a fight, presumably with a pack of raptors, several of which it had killed. The bodies of the raptors did not bear the institute's brand and were significantly smaller than the breed kept in the animal pens above. Suspecting intruders, we went back to search the chambers.

Perhaps because of their injuries, or perhaps some other reason, the outlaws surrendered after only a token fight. The remainder of their raptor pack we tranquilized and transported with the leftover supplies that we found in the laboratory.

Chapter Three

[1162.07.10]

So, it's come to pass. After sixteen years of toiling in the Justice Ministry—sixteen years of shit work, sixteen years of breaking open cases only to see the credit go to someone else, sixteen years of watching the pale-skinned and pretty gain favor at my expense—after sixteen years of concentrated horse piss from the higher-ups, I've finally been made principal investigator on a case of my own. Cause for celebration, right? I should slaughter some pigs and break out the wine, invite the whole damn neighborhood to the party.

But I'm no fool. I've spent long enough dodging the arrows of Protectorate malice to see this for what it is: a giant, gold-plated turd. For one thing, this investigation should be massive. Dozens of Tensors died in the disaster. Short of wars and terrorist attacks, this is the deadliest incident that's befallen both the Tensorate and the Protectorate in decades. Yet they've assigned just me to work on the investigation, some mid-ranking Tensor who's never handled her own case before. And while I'd like to think that my years of successes are being rewarded—who unmasked the Cashewnut killer? Who exposed the ring of naga breeders at the heart of the Tensorate?—I am nowhere that naive. Some agenda is at work here. Corruption rises from this affair like corpse-gas from a murky lake, stinking of putrefying secrets.

The Rewar Teng institute has been plagued by scandal and rumor since its inception. Nobody buys that they built a whole research institute out in the mountains just to stitch together better livestock. At the very least, there's some shifty experimentation going on up there. And then there are the wilder tales: human sacrifices, mad attempts to deform the shape of the world. Is there any truth to these rumors? Who the fuck knows. All I know—all any of us peons know—is that everything to do with the institute is sewn up so tight, you could be sent to the mines just for asking.

So, something in the institute has gone belly-up and they want to conceal it. That's what this is. They've picked me, some nobody with no prospects and no future, to be their puppet or, if anything sour surfaces during the investigation, their sacrificial goat. A hapless Kebangilan orphan whose adoptive family never liked her. Someone who's bound to be so afraid of exile, she'll do anything the Protectorate asks.

Idiots. They should have done their research, because I am not that person. I didn't get to where I am today by playing the good girl and keeping my head below the grass. Whatever they're trying to hide, I will find it. I will make them regret underestimating me.

The stress is getting to me, though. I won't lie about that. This morning, I woke with my head ringing and my clothes clinging to my skin. Some slime-fish of a nightmare, slipping away the moment you try to hold it in your memory, growing dimmer the more you flail at its shape. There was something about a cave with tall ceilings, and a strange girl talking to me. Large pools of water, just like from my childhood. Except that I never lived near water in my childhood. We were hillside farmers. There was only the old mine, and children weren't allowed down there. It was just a silly dream, a conjuration of a stressed mind, but I've spent the entire day with a prickle gathered around the skin of my neck. Every time I remember the husk of that dream, I shiver. Small things that shouldn't bother me set my mind off like a firework. The slap of water on floor tiles sounds like footsteps. The creak of wood cooling at night sends my heart racing.

Earlier this evening, I thought I heard someone whispering outside my window, but when I ran to check, there was no one there. Am I losing my mind?

Curse it all. It doesn't help that I'm alone in this house. It would be nice if my pay allowed me to hire servants, but of course it doesn't. And it would be wonderful if Kayan were here, but of course she isn't. That's what I get for marrying the daughter of a pirate queen—I see her three times a year, and that's it. It's fine. She'd only mock me for getting worked up by a meaningless dream, anyway.

Well. Journey of a thousand steps, and all that. I've sent for the chief investigator from the southern provinces—Ngiau Chimin. Don't like her. She's the kind of sadistic vampire who drinks power from the veins of the Protectorate. The bastard is drunk on her bloody authority. But she's good at interrogations. Once might almost say, too good. <u>She</u> can talk to the outlaws, considering that I wasn't allowed any access to them—a fantastic start to things. I'm sure she'll get something useful out of them. She's got a reputation to maintain.

Chapter Four

Most esteemed Tensor Yesai:

Greetings, and may the threads of fortune bring you blessings. No doubt you are aware of who I am, being that I have taken charge of the investigation into the Rewar Teng incident.

First of all, I must commend you on your excellent report. It is thanks to your foresight and your fortitude that we have so much valuable information to begin our investigations with. For that I can only offer you my deepest gratitude.

Knowing what you have endured in your foray to the institute, I must humbly beg for your further assistance. There are questions about what happened in the caverns beneath the institute, questions which are crucial to our understanding of the sequence of events, questions which have not been answered by the information I have been given so far. I suspect you could help me immensely with answering these questions. After all, you were at the institute in person, and you witnessed its state with your own two eyes. There is no one else who knows the situation like you do. Tensor Yesai, I would like to interview you in person, at your earliest convenience. Please let me know when this can be arranged.

Tensor Chuwan Sariman

———————

Tensor Sariman:

I appreciate the letter you have sent to me. Unfortunately, I am not authorized to speak directly to someone of your seniority. I must ask that you send your questions to my superior in this matter, High Tensor Fang Bing.

Tensor Yesai

———————

Tensor Sariman:

It has come to my attention that you have questions about certain omissions that were made in the report submitted by Tensor Yesai to your investigation. Yes, indeed there were omissions made. Yes, we are aware of such omissions. I assure you that they were made deliberately, with the full knowledge of the relevant authorities. There is far more at stake here than your petty investigation into an industrial accident. Information has been withheld for the sake of the safety and security of the Protectorate.

If you understand the import of this, then I hope you will trouble yourself no further by continuing to chase smoke down dead men's intestines.

High Tensor Fang Bing

Most esteemed High Tensor:

I have received your letter and I understand the meaning contained therein, although I confess that I do not understand its purpose. Perhaps I am not meant to; after all, I am only a lowly insect doing the bidding of the Protectorate.

Allow me to ask, however—by whose authorization were these facts withheld?

Your most humble servant,
Chuwan Sariman

———————

MEMO FROM CHUWAN'S NOTEBOOK

Well, fuck. Looks like they're making this as difficult for me as possible. Cheebye.

They're mistaken if they think this will stop me.

Chapter Five

PROGRESS REPORT FOR THE INCIDENT AT THE REWAR
TENG INSTITUTE OF EXPERIMENTAL METHODS

PREPARED BY TENSOR CHUWAN SARIMAN

This report summarizes the progress that has been made as of this third day of the investigation into the incident at the Rewar Teng Institute of Experimental Methods. So far, the investigation has proceeded much slower than I would prefer. There have been many delays and obstacles, some administrative, others less quantifiable.

The technicians have completed their examination of the crossbreed recovered from the institute. Their conclusions are in agreement with Tensor Yesai's initial assessment: that the creature was an albino cross between a raptor and a naga. It was well fed and in good health when it died, although the technicians noted that the creature's lack of pigmentation was not genetic but appeared to be a chronic stress response. I do not know if this constitutes evidence that the institute staff mistreated their animals, but I do know that whatever this creature was, it was not happy.

I requested an interview with Tensor Yesai to further elaborate on the issues raised in her report. However, I was told in the strongest possible terms that I was not to query further in this direction, and that such instructions came from higher up the Protectorate hierarchy than I have access to. I do not intend to pursue this line of inquiry any further; I merely wanted this to go on the record.

The assessment of the staff's personal effects has yielded little of use, in the most troubling ways. It is strange that the recovered items spanned the range of clothing and light captures and books, but there were no diaries or letters amongst them. We have recovered no personal writings of any of the forty-two staff of the institute. This creates a significant gap in our understanding of the day-to-day proceedings of the institute, which is in turn a significant obstacle to our understanding of the environment and working atmosphere therein. While the laboratory logbooks are an extensive and meticulous record of the experiments conducted, they give no insight into the operations of the institute otherwise. What did the Tensors stationed there do for leisure? How did the stresses of isolation affect them? Were they happy working there, or was there discontent which may have fueled something more? These questions, and more, remain intractably opaque.

On a more positive note, the medical examiner has declared that the outlaws are sufficiently recovered from their injuries to attend the interrogations. I have assigned Tensor N to begin at once, tomorrow. If they prove cooperative, their testimony could be the axle around which this investigation pivots.

————————

Tensor Sariman:

An excellent report. Your concerns about the investigation are noted. Proceed in whatever way you can. Remember that the families of the victims are waiting upon you to give your final report, so that they may let the memories of their loved ones rest. Do not let them down.

Senior Tensor Mikao

Chapter Six

[1162.07.13]

Fuck them all. Burn them to ashes and scatter them in the sewers. There's a point where willful incompetence crosses over into outright malice, and these gravefuckers have sailed right over that threshold. "Do not let them down"—just cut me in half with a bone saw. You don't care about the families of the victims. You just want me to close the investigation with minimal effort put in. Whatever truth there is hidden here, you want it buried so deep, its bones petrify in the airless dark. This charade is worse than if they'd plainly told me "submit a moldering heap of cow dung, because we don't care if you do your job properly." Their pretense toward decency and fairness leaves a far fouler taste. Fuck them all. Chao cheebye.

They won't stop me. It'll take more than letter-writing games to intimidate me. So, they've purged information from Tensor Yesai's report and won't let me talk to her. I'll find it some other way. Ngiau Chimin is hard at work. I'll lean on her.

In the secrecy of my head, I'm starting to make terrible, worst-case-scenario plans. What if I quit the ministry and continue the investigation privately? Could I become an outlaw, pursued to the ends of the Protectorate by vengeful Tensors? Kayan would be delighted, her pure snowdrop following her path into villainy and infamy. At least we would get to spend more time together, right?

No, I'm losing my grip on what's real and what's not. The nightmares that started when I got this job have not eased—in fact, they are worse than ever. I woke last night from the middle of a sweat-thick terror. People I couldn't see had me chained to a metal table, and there was a thick, sharp needle pressed into my head, boring through my skull. I could feel the vibrations in my jawbone and teeth. The pressure in my skull. I woke with a terrible pain in my stomach and a memory of sensations so sharp, I could not believe they hadn't been real—the coppery cold of metal against skin, the eruption of violence within my skull. It took me more than ten minutes to convince myself it had just been a dream, and most of a sun-cycle before I could fall back asleep again. All day, I've imagined human voices in the wordless song of the wind or the distant passage of a cart. When I turn my head, sometimes I see brief flashes of light, as if something at the periphery of my vision had caught fire. It's as if I'm being haunted by these dreams.

It's really nothing, and I feel a fool for being so affected by these silly tricks of the mind, but I'm increasingly anxious all the time. Today, I shouted at Lau Niang when she startled me cleaning the office, and she really did not deserve that. She just works here and has to put up with all the nonsense Tensors deal her. The stress is turning me into the kind of person I loathe.

I wish Kayan were here. I can afford to be sentimental because she isn't around to mock me for it.

Chapter Seven

Tensor Sariman:

Please find enclosed the transcript of Tensor Ngiau's interrogation of the female outlaw, self-identified as Rider. Tensorate records link this individual to the now-disgraced person Tan Khimyan, but she has been part of the terrorist rebel movement for the past three years. Our knowledge of her existence is merely circumstantial, however, and she should be treated with caution. The investigating agents assigned to the Bataanar incident tell us that she is a Quarterlander who rides a naga mount, expert at dealing with such creatures. Take that as you will.

The High Overseer of Magistrates
Ministry of Justice

High Overseer:

Thank you for this report. I wonder, though, if some mistake has been made? Not only is the report incomplete, but crucial sections of it appear to have been removed.

Tensor Sariman

Tensor:

It is what it is.

The High Overseer of Magistrates

Chapter Eight

PRISONER INTERROGATION TRANSCRIPT

[1162.07.14]

BEING THE TRANSCRIPT OF THE QUESTIONING CON-
DUCTED BY TENSOR NGIAU CHIMIN OF THE PRISONER
KNOWN AS "RIDER," IN RELATION TO THE INVESTIGA-
TION INTO THE DISASTER AT REWAR TENG

Tensor N: You must know why you're here.

R: ████████████████████████████████████

Tensor N: We want to know what you did.

R: We did nothing. No, that's not entirely true. We did kill
the beast. But it attacked us first. Everything else was dead
when we arrived.

Tensor N: Don't lie to me. We know who you are.

R: Do you? Sometimes, it feels like I don't know who I am.

Tensor N: Oh, you think you're funny. We know who your friends are. Are you aware how much of your treasonous behavior is punishable by death?

R: All of it, I assume. Is this why you have called me here? So you can offer to spare my life in exchange for information?

Tensor N: Things will go easier for you if you cooperate. For you, and for your partner. His wounds are serious. Don't you think he needs a doctor? Listen. I know your type. You don't seem violent. Just fell in with the wrong crowd, didn't you? I've seen many cases like yours before. These rebels, these terrorists, they start off pretending to be your friends, offering you help and support. Before you know it, they've become your only help and support. You can't escape. You're trapped. But it doesn't have to be this way. We can help you leave. Let us.

R: I just have to tell you what happened?

Tensor N: Just tell us everything.

R: And all this will be on the record? Your assistant—he is writing this down?

Tensor N: Yes. Does that worry you?

R: It does not. Very well. I will tell you all that I know.

Tensor N: I knew you would be reasonable. Let's start. What brought you to the institute?

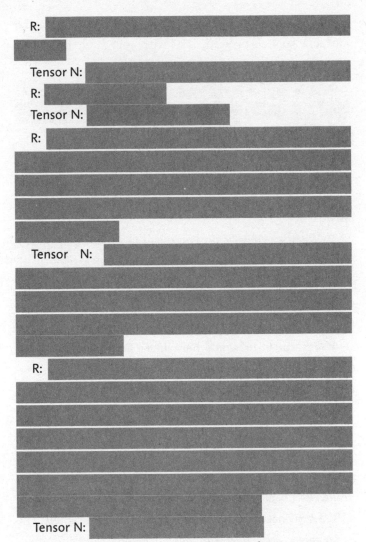

R: It is indeed. Unfortunately, also one that is true.

Tensor N: All right, if you want to go with that story, we

will put it on record. Perhaps a plea of insanity will save your life. Let's go step by step. Start with your approach to the institute.

R: ███████████████████████████████████████
██
███████████████████████

Tensor N: Who's "we"?

R: Myself and my partner. Mokoya.

Tensor N: The Protector's daughter? Is she involved in this as well?

R: What specifically do you mean by "this"? She was involved in helping me look for my sibling. That is all.

Tensor N: Of course. Sure. Please continue.

R: Bramble was hurt—

Tensor N: Your naga. Am I right?

R: Yes, she is. I rescued her when I lived in the Quarterlands. The two of us have—

Tensor N: So, you're an expert on these creatures, aren't you?

R: I . . . I know Bramble. I took her in and raised her when she was a fledgling. I cannot speak for the wild ones.

Tensor N: Of course. A convenient excuse. Please, continue. Your naga was hurt. What then?

R: I convinced Mokoya to stay behind with Bramble. She is pregnant, and had been feeling ill recently.

Tensor N: She let you go on your own? I find that difficult

to believe. You can barely walk unassisted.

R: It is what happened.

Tensor N: You convinced her.

R: Yes. And then I left. I traveled across the bleeding plains that separate Rewar Teng from the mountain path.

Tensor N: What about Sanao Akeha? Did he not accompany you?

R: They came later. Mokoya sent them after me.

Tensor N: Describe your journey. What happened? What did you see?

R: It was mostly rocks and trees, very desolate and strange. It took me a day and a half to cross the plains. It was exhausting.

Tensor N: Did you see anyone during that time? Any animals?

R: It was all bones, some older than the others. No. There was one—I saw an animal from afar, but something killed it by the time I got closer to the institute. There were only pieces left.

Tensor N: What was it?

R: I do not know. Some kind of hybrid animal, half insect, half fawn. Your Tensorate should have better records than I do. I believe their beast killed it. ███████████

████████████████████████████

███████████████

Tensor N: Keep talking. Tell me what happened next.

R: I approached the institute as sunfall was approaching. In hindsight, not knowing what awaited me, I should have waited until next sunrise to enter the institute. But I was tired from traveling. I did not think rationally. I could only see the glistening end to my arduous journey. I could only think of the answers to all of my questions.

Tensor N: ███████████████████

R: ████████████████████████████

████████████████████████████████

████████████████████████████████

██████████████████████████

Tensor N: ████████████████

R: ████████████████████████████████

██████████████████████████

Tensor N: ███████████████████

████████████████████████████████

███████████████████████

R: ████████████████████████████

███████████████

Tensor N: Tell me what you saw when you broke in.

R: I saw death. The institute was abandoned and the courtyard was full of bones and half-eaten bodies.

Tensor N: What did you do then?

R: I went into the dormitories first. I wanted to see if someone might have survived, by some miracle. But there was nothing except broken things and dead bodies.

Tensor N: I want you to describe the scene in detail.

R: I don't remember it well. I wrote it down as I went, because I could not grasp the horror of what I was seeing. The kitchen was on the ground floor, as was the dining area. I looked there first. Everything had been knocked over, there was dirt all over the floor, broken utensils, raw vegetables that were rotting. There was blood too, old and dried. I didn't find anything useful. Then—then I went upstairs.

Tensor N:

R:

Tensor N:

R:

Tensor N:

R:

Tensor N:

R:

Tensor N:

R:

Tensor N:

R:

Tensor N:

R:

Tensor N:

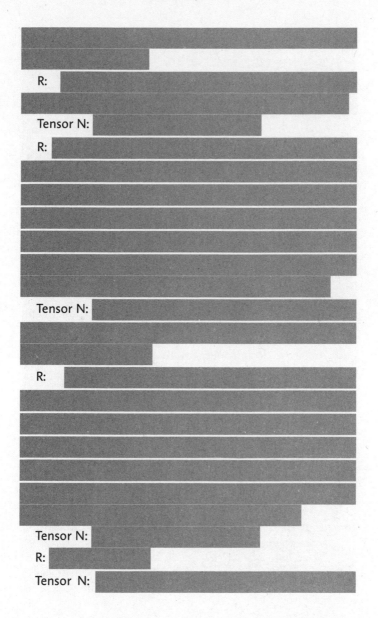

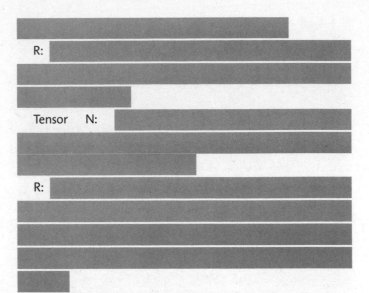

Tensor N: You're wasting my time. Move on. What happened next?

R: After the dormitories, I went to the laboratory building. I could hear something moving around the buildings, but I didn't see anything. It made me more cautious. Something had broken the door in; it was a big metal door, the height of two floors. I thought the creature might be sleeping in there, but I went inside anyway. Thankfully, the laboratory was unoccupied. Just some tanks and empty cages. Maybe a few dead animals. Some Tensors had definitely died there, but the creature must have dragged the bodies outside.

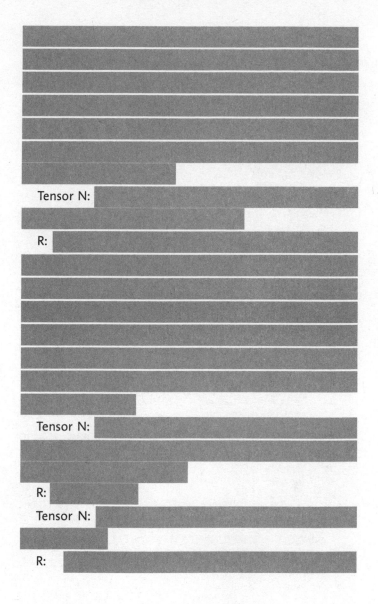

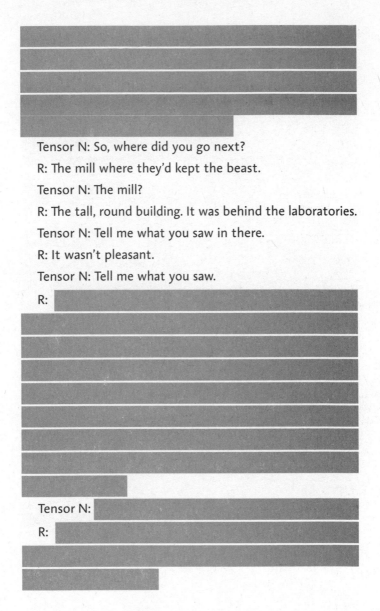

Tensor N: So, where did you go next?

R: The mill where they'd kept the beast.

Tensor N: The mill?

R: The tall, round building. It was behind the laboratories.

Tensor N: Tell me what you saw in there.

R: It wasn't pleasant.

Tensor N: Tell me what you saw.

R:

Tensor N:

R:

Tensor N: What did you do?

R: I ran back outside.

Tensor N: Into the courtyard with all the dead bodies?

R: The air there was open.

Tensor N: You didn't enter the main institute building?

R: I did, after visiting the animal pens.

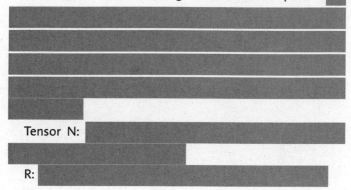

Tensor N:

R:

Chapter Nine

[1162.07.14]

Are they joking? Why bother giving me a transcript that's half blacked out? I can't do anything with this rubbish. Save your time and my stomach bile and send nothing at all. Cheebye. I can't deal with these people.

I'm exhausted, to be honest. When the transcript was delivered to me today, I felt like throwing it across the room and going straight to bed. Pathetic, I know, but the obstacles before me feel less like a wall and more like a mountain range, cloud-topped and impassable. What's the point of throwing myself against it, over and over? I will break against its side and the mountain will feel nothing. My bones will crumble into dust at its feet and it will remain. It's injustice in its purest form, and I almost want to give up. Why should I waste my life and my happiness on this doomed endeavor? I should retire and become a farmer like my parents. (My real parents, not the guilty strangers who took me off the streets and pretended that their money made them good caretakers.)

Nightmares haven't abated. I get the one about the needle in my head, and then another one where this old Tensor forces me to take a strange test. There was a fishpond, and I had to make all the fish swim in a particular way, or I would be in trouble. Then there are the formless nightmares, a mix of things that happened in the past day melded with things I thought <u>might</u> have happened but didn't. None of them make sense when I wake up. I always feel like I've been drowned, and I have to convince myself I'm still alive. When I close my eyes, I can still see fish dancing in little circles on the skin of my eyelids.

I don't understand. How can these watery, mundane dreams make me feel upset and unsafe the entire day? They're not even about scary things. I mean, fish swimming and the disapproval of teachers? I've investigated murderers and sadists. The things that give <u>other</u> people nightmares don't faze me. Is it exhaustion? Is someone poisoning me, turning my mind into boneless mush?

It's a funny thing, isn't it? The last time my path crossed the female outlaw's, it was because of illegal experiments conducted in the shadows, hidden in the dark pockets at the center of the Protectorate. Different people's shit, same delightful stink. I'm not even upset anymore. How else will the Tensorate continue to disappoint me?

[1162.07.15]

Fucking gravefuckers. I guess I have my answer.

Chapter Ten

*I demand an explanation! What incompetence could
allow two prisoners to escape from one of the most se-
cure facilities in the Protectorate? Two prisoners involved in an active investigation, no less! My critical
investigation hinged upon them, and you let them escape? What have you to say for yourself?*

Tensor Sariman

———————

Tensor:

*We have no excuses, no explanation adequate for the
depth of our failure! A thousand years would not be
enough to exculpate us from our wrongs. We place*

our lives at the mercy of the Protector, from whom we can only beg the greatest of forgivenesses.

The prisoners have escaped. The details of how still elude us, but it is clear they had outside help. Something was slipped into the guards' wine in the kitchen, some sort of sleeping draft. As the night went on, more and more of them fell asleep, which is how the prisoners made their escape with the minimum of bloodshed. A pity! It would have been far preferable to die honorably stopping them!

While we cannot conclusively name the collaborator, the fugitives made their getaway on a naga (which we assume belonged to the prisoner Rider), which can only mean the rescuer was one of her close associates.

I am sorry to report the passing of Tensor Ngiau, who had been living in the facility for the duration of the investigation. She was found with her throat slit, and this note from Sanao Akeha was left in her room. I think the conclusions we can draw are painfully obvious.

Overseer Tan
Ministry of Justice

THE NOTE FOUND BESIDE NGIAU CHIMIN'S BODY

You should thank the fortunes, or whatever deity you believe in, that my sister planned the rescue. If it had been me, I would have left a sea of bodies from wall to wall.

S.A.

Chapter Eleven

Most Honored Minister:

It is to my greatest dismay that I must report a fatal disruption to the investigation of the Rewar Teng Incident. I have no doubt that you have already heard of the escape of the two suspects we had in our custody, the terrorists Sanao Akeha and his female companion, Rider.

I write to you in this moment to request assistance. These two outlaws are crucial to the completion of the investigation. Only they know the truth of what happened at the institute, and I have yet to extract that truth from them. I humbly beg you to grant me the authority to hunt these fugitives. Grant me jurisdiction across the length and breadth of the Protectorate.

Yours most humbly,
Tensor Chuwan Sariman

———————

My dearest Chuwan:

Blame the fortunes, who conspire to put you in such a terrible situation! You were doing well in the investigation, but it cannot be helped. These outlaws cannot be contained. I know Akeha well—I raised him as a child, and I am not in the least surprised by his despicable actions.

This turn of events makes it clear who was truly responsible for the disaster at Rewar Teng. Do we need any more proof of their guilt than the fact that they have fled from justice, leaving more victims in their wake? The families of the forty-two who died at Rewar Teng must have their answers, Chuwan. You know this as well as I do. We may not be able to draw the truth from the mouths of the reprobates ourselves, but we can at least give these grieving citizens a semblance of closure. Do what you can. Send in your final report.

Fear not. You have done an exemplary job in these difficult circumstances. I will see that you are rewarded accordingly when this is all over.

Minister Sanao Sonami

Chapter Twelve

[1162.07.19]

What do you do after you've made the worst decision in your life? Spend two days in a drunken stupor, shirking work and chasing away anyone who comes to your door, apparently. Regrets? Too many to list.

I did it. I caved to Protectorate pressure and drafted a fake investigation report, just like they wanted. How could anyone say no to Minister Sonami, a favored daughter of the Protector herself? Not this coward, obviously. Soon, an official decree will be issued declaring the investigation closed. The families of those who perished at the institute will have their answer. They will know to place the deaths of their loved ones upon the heads of those wicked, evil, no-good terrorist rebels, those saboteurs who invaded the institute and released the great beast that devoured everything in its path. Their anger will be reshaped into righteousness in the service of the Protectorate, their hearts rededicated to the cause of eradicating this blight from the bright rivers and the gentle green of the land. And I? I will of course receive my reward in due time for my role in this great orchestra. As promised by Minister Sanao.

Who cares if that is not what happened? Who cares if the truth has been strangled and buried in an unmarked grave? Who cares, as long as it all serves the needs of the Protectorate? None of my fucking business anymore, is it? I put my seal on it and sent it away. The families of the dead will have their answer. The soulless void of the high Tensorate has been appeased. I can turn my back on this as it sinks into the obscurity of history. In ten years, a hundred years, who will remember what happened here?

Fuck this all. I'll never look Kayan in the eye again. I can't. I haven't even dared write her. I know what she'd say. However disappointed I am in myself, she'd be ten times more. And I deserve it. What was I thinking? What the fuck was I thinking?

Chapter Thirteen

[1162.07.20]

Upsetting day. More so than usual, which says a lot. I was ambushed as I was leaving the Halls of Justice. It was dark—I'd stayed late doing busywork, the details of which have been entirely purged from my mind. I was walking past that row of peony bushes that line the path and litter it with slippery flowers. A white hand shot out and seized my wrist. Of course I screamed, and a second hand clamped itself over my mouth. My mind went blank. I was sure I was going to be murdered. So much for all that Tensorate training! When it came to the crisis point, all I'd learned was for nothing. I couldn't open my mindeye. I couldn't see the Slack. All I could think was "I can't die <u>now</u>." I froze up like a fawn in the talons of a naga. No—worse, actually. At least fawns kick.

The person who grabbed me was a woman, broad-shouldered and dressed like a worker. She didn't introduce herself at first, and in my panic, I thought she was a demon, a jiangshi, the angry spirit of one of the institute dead, come to take revenge. Wild thoughts consumed me.

She asked, "Are you Tensor Chuwan Sariman?" In my fear, I couldn't think of a lie that would save my life, so I nodded like a damn fool.

Her name was Cai Yuan-ning, and her brother Cai Yuanfang had died in the institute. I remembered his name. He had been the youngest member of the staff, a mere twenty-four.

The madness I saw in Yuan-ning was not a devouring inferno of vengeance, untamable by reason. Rather, it was a furnace—desperation burning bright and terrible, driving her forward. "Your report is wrong," she kept saying. When I pressed her about what she meant, she said, "There's more you don't know."

How naive did she think I was? I was frankly insulted she thought she needed to tell me this. By that time, I had calmed down a little, but not entirely. And in that dangerous zone—the heartbeat-sharp floodplain between animal panic and cold rationality—I decided she was worth questioning anyway. "So, tell me. What do you have that I don't?"

She got nervous then, licking her lips, struggling for words. I could see her regretting the choices she'd made coming here. But she had my attention, and I wasn't going to let her go so easily. "What did you come to tell me?"

She leaned toward me. "Did you read my brother's letters? Did you see what we discussed?"

I told her there were no letters. No journals, no personal writings from any of the staff. I told her the Tensors who swept the institute found nothing. "Either they were destroyed, or someone else took them." Foul lies. I am rock-certain that the Tensorate was hiding these letters from all of us.

"No letters? That's not possible," she said.

I grabbed her hand. "Tell me what was in those letters. You must have kept the ones he sent you. Where are they?"

She tried to pull away. I tightened my grip. The tides had turned: now I was the hunter, and she the soft morsel in flight. I assailed her with questions. What had her brother told her? What did he know? Had he seen something that shouldn't have been there?

"I'm sorry, I don't know," she stuttered. "Please, don't kill me."

Her words jarred me out of the fit I'd fallen into. I wasn't going to hurt her—what an absurd thought!—but she didn't know that. She was a peasant, and peasants are raised to fear Tensors. I should know: I used to be a peasant too.

Guilt slapped me. I was fighting her when we should have been natural allies.

This dive into decency cost me. The moment I spent feeling remorse undid my focus, and Yuan-ning took full advantage. She jerked from my grasp and ran.

I shouted after her. She sped up in panic, fleeing down the white stone of the path. But then something happened that I swear must have been decreed by the fortunes: I fell. I tripped over something on the ground, but there was nothing there. And maybe I can blame my bad nerves, but I've never fallen like that in my life—ever!—so why would I start now?

By the time I regained my footing, Yuan-ning was gone. Which was just as well, because two guards arrived, alerted by my shouting. They were very concerned. If Yuan-ning had been there still, she would have been arrested on the spot. As it was, I told the guards that I had been startled by a cobra slipping into the grass. Searching for it kept them occupied for long enough.

I don't know where Yuan-ning went. I don't know what she wanted to tell me. Idiot. If only I'd stopped to listen.

I came home and drank half a bottle of rice wine and

lost myself to sleep for an entire sun-cycle. Of course I had another strange dream. This time, the ghost my mind chose was Yuwen, my roommate from the Academy. I haven't thought about her in years: a fussy, watery girl with thin wrists and no convictions. She was saying, over and over, as she poured red liquid into a cup, "Things will go where they like. But you can change the flow." What the fuck did that mean?

The sun has come and gone since I woke from that dream, and those words are still looping in my mind like a siren. Like the call of the gravesent birds that wake me at first sunrise every morning.

I keep running the encounter with Cai Yuan-ning through my head, and I can't shake the thought that her sudden appearance—and fortuitous getaway—are connected to these strange dreams I'm having. It makes no literal, material sense, but every time I think of one and then the other, something clicks pleasingly into place in my mind. Maybe it's instinct at work here, or all the years I've spent picking puzzles apart. My unconscious mind sees patterns before my rational self notices them.

Or maybe I'm being sent a message. Maybe something or someone is telling me that the investigation is not done yet. Some kind of bizarre, unknowable slackcraft is being used to plant ideas and images in my head, to manipulate the fabric of the world so that strange things keep tumbling into my path. But who would be capable of doing this, and what do they want? Whose side are they on?

I just reread that entire last paragraph. It sounds like the ravings of a madwoman. And that madwoman is me.

Time for more rice wine, I think.

[SOME HOURS LATER]

Mad as it is, I can't shake that line of thought. I think I know what I must do.

I'll never get peace otherwise.

Chapter Fourteen

[1162.07.21]

So, this is what it's like to be an outlaw. All the songs play up the excitement, the adventure, the nobility of convictions. What a joke. All I feel is stressed out and anxious, and toweringly stupid. Out of my depth.

But I did it. I broke into what used to be Tensor Ngiau's office and stole those gravesent transcripts so I could see what they were trying to hide. All it took was staying late in the compound and slipping through gaps in the guards' attentions. Don't act like this is some kind of great achievement, Sariman.

How I found the transcripts was a matter of miracles. There's this ornate incense burner in Tensor Ngiau's office. When I got in, a massive stack of papers was in the barrel, charcoal-black but still crawling with worms of red fire at the edges. I still don't know what drove me to do it, but I put the fire out. Good thing I'm not completely useless at slackcraft. When I peeled the charred contents of the barrel apart, I found the transcripts at its heart, charred around the edges but still intact. See? Miracles, as I said. I don't know how or why those papers in particular were spared, but they were.

What sloppiness on the part of the Tensorate. I mean, if they'd truly wanted to destroy all evidence about the institute, the absolutely could have. But they didn't even try. The way this looked to me, they were just disposing of trash, burning the clutter in Ngiau's room. They clearly did not think anyone would be searching for this now that the official investigation has been closed.

So, hubris, then.

In any case, I have the transcripts and I've read them. My first reaction: vindication. My second reaction: Horror and fury. I'm only slightly ashamed to say I felt vindication first. But I <u>was</u> right; what went on in that institute was fucked up as a pig's ass. No wonder those <u>bastards</u> wanted to keep this under wraps. And it's only half a transcript, too. Which means there was worse than what I read. Great Slack, what were they up to in that dark, breeding humans? Murdering children?

Now I have to find out. But my flash of bravery (or madness) is over, and in its wake, it's clear that I don't have a plan. In fact, I never had one. I don't even know what I should do with these gravesent transcripts. Should I destroy them? Erase all evidence of my guilt and remain a good girl in the eyes of the Protectorate? It's not too late to turn back. I haven't done anything irreversible. I could still drop this surreptitious investigation and pretend none of this ever happened. Go back to my gilded life with a tight smile on my face.

Who am I trying to fool. Of course I'm keeping these. Maybe at some point in the future, they'll be important evidence. Maybe I'll get to accuse someone of great evildoing and this will be what seals their fate. But for now, the next step is to follow these transcripts where they lead. And I have some ideas.

Chapter Fifteen

Ngiau never sent this one to me. I wonder why.

[*1162.07.14*]

BEING THE TRANSCRIPT OF THE QUESTIONING CON-
DUCTED BY TENSOR NGIAU CHIMIN OF THE PRISONER
SANAO AKEHA, IN RELATION TO THE INVESTIGATION
INTO THE DISASTER AT REWAR TENG

Tensor N: This is a pleasure. How often does my job bring
me face-to-face with one of the most notorious criminals in
the Protectorate? I'm frankly surprised by the scale of your
crimes this time. I had thought you could be redeemed. I
have a certain fondness for you, after all. You probably don't

remember me, Akeha, but I remember you and your sister. I watched you from afar, when we both lived in the Great High Palace. Do you remember that?

SA: . . .

Tensor N: Not going to talk? We have many creative methods to get people to speak up, Akeha. Would you like to try them out?

SA: If you want to waste your time and effort, go ahead.

Tensor N: This is not an empty threat, Akeha. I haven't constructed my reputation as an expert interrogator out of nothing. I'm sure you know.

SA: What did you expect? That I would fall to my knees, beg for your mercy, and tell you everything?

Tensor N: No, I expected you to act like the arrogant brat you are—

SA: A brat? You would call me a brat? You, that parasitic grub clinging to favor in my mother's palace?

Tensor N: Ah, so you do remember me.

SA: You had one friend back then. Didn't you? One of the serving boys. Daisun.

Tensor N: You—

SA: He was a pretty morsel, whom you liked more than he liked you. And then something happened. Daisun became a walking ghost. He wouldn't eat and wouldn't talk to people. He wouldn't say what was wrong. Then he disappeared.

Tensor N: You dare?

SA: What did you do with his body?

Tensor N: You are accusing me of a serious crime.

SA: You thought no one knew, but I did—

Tensor N: I don't take these accusations lightly.

SA: Haah. You can try to deny—aah. You know, I quite like pain. Ah.

Tensor N: Get him out of here.

Chapter Sixteen

PRISONER INTERROGATION TRANSCRIPT

[1162.07.14]

**BEING THE TRANSCRIPT OF THE QUESTIONING CON-
DUCTED BY TENSOR NGIAU CHIMIN OF THE PRISONER
KNOWN AS "RIDER," IN RELATION TO THE INVESTIGA-
TION INTO THE DISASTER AT REWAR TENG**

Tensor N: You must know why you're here.

R: You want to know what we saw down there, in the institute.

Tensor N: We want to know what you did.

R: We did nothing. No, that's not entirely true. We did kill the beast. But it attacked us first. Everything else was dead when we arrived.

Tensor N: Don't lie to me. We know who you are.

R: Do you? Sometimes, it feels like I don't know who I am.

Tensor N: Oh, you think you're funny. We know who your friends are. Are you aware how much of your treasonous behavior is punishable by death?

R: All of it, I assume. Is this why you have called me here? So you can offer to spare my life in exchange for information?

Tensor N: Things will go easier for you if you cooperate. For you, and for your partner. His wounds are serious. Don't you think he needs a doctor? Listen. I know your type. You don't seem violent. Just fell in with the wrong crowd, didn't you? I've seen many cases like yours before. These rebels, these terrorists, they start off pretending to be your friends, offering you help and support. Before you know it, they've become your only help and support. You can't escape. You're trapped. But it doesn't have to be this way. We can help you leave. Let us.

R: I just have to tell you what happened?

Tensor N: Just tell us everything.

R: And all this will be on the record? Your assistant—he is writing this down?

Tensor N: Yes. Does that worry you?

R: It does not. Very well. I will tell you all that I know.

Tensor N: I knew you would be reasonable. Let's start. What brought you to the institute?

R: I was looking for my sibling. My twin.

Tensor N: Your twin? What was her name?

R: I don't know.

Tensor N: You don't know?

R: We were separated at birth. I do not know their name—if your people named them at all. They were one of your experimental subjects at the institute.

Tensor N: Your sister was a goat? Or is your naga a cousin? The only experimental subjects at the institute were the animals being bred there.

R: No, you Tensors experimented on children in the caverns below the institute. They lived there. Do not look so surprised, Tensor—your investigators found me there. They saw what was hidden in the rock. The pods and the living cells—

Tensor N: A ludicrous story.

R: It is indeed. Unfortunately, also one that is true.

Tensor N: All right, if you want to go with that story, we will put it on record. Perhaps a plea of insanity will save your life. Let's go step by step. Start with your approach to the institute.

R: I came on foot. We traveled north on Bramble, my naga, but she got hurt in the bad weather, and—

Tensor N: Who's "we"?

R: Myself and my partner. Mokoya.

Tensor N: The Protector's daughter? Is she involved in this as well?

R: What specifically do you mean by "this"? She was involved in helping me look for my sibling. That is all.

Tensor N: Of course. Sure. Please continue.

R: Bramble was hurt—

Tensor N: Your naga. Am I right?

R: Yes, she is. I rescued her when I lived in the Quarterlands. The two of us have—

Tensor N: So, you're an expert on these creatures, aren't you?

R: I . . . I know Bramble. I took her in and raised her when she was a fledgling. I cannot speak for the wild ones.

Tensor N: Of course. A convenient excuse. Please, continue. Your naga was hurt. What then?

R: I convinced Mokoya to stay behind with Bramble. She is pregnant and had been feeling ill recently.

Tensor N: She let you go on your own? I find that difficult to believe. You can barely walk unassisted.

R: It is what happened.

Tensor N: You convinced her.

R: Yes. And then I left. I traveled across the bleeding plains that separate Rewar Teng from the mountain path.

Tensor N: What about Sanao Akeha? Did he not accompany you?

R: They came later. Mokoya sent them after me.

Tensor N: Describe your journey. What happened? What did you see?

R: It was mostly rocks and trees, very desolate and strange. It took me a day and a half to cross the plains. It was exhausting.

Tensor N: Did you see anyone during that time? Any animals?

R: It was all bones, some older than the others. No. There was one—I saw an animal from afar, but something killed it by the time I got closer to the institute. There were only pieces left.

Tensor N: What was it?

R: I do not know. Some kind of hybrid animal, half insect, half fawn. Your Tensorate should have better records than I do. I believe their beast killed it. You know which one I speak of, do you not? The naga crossbreed.

Tensor N: Keep talking. Tell me what happened next.

R: I approached the institute as sunfall was approaching. In hindsight, not knowing what awaited me, I should have waited until next sunrise to enter the institute. But I was tired from traveling. I did not think rationally. I could only see the glistening end to my arduous journey. I could only think of the answers to all of my questions.

Tensor N: So you just walked in?

R: It wasn't guarded. There was a barrier, but it had decayed. The institute must have been abandoned for days.

Tensor N: It wasn't abandoned.

R: Some people had clearly left. Others were not so lucky.

Tensor N: All the institute staff perished in the incident. No one survived. No one got away.

R: If that comforts you, then go on believing it.

Tensor N: Tell me what you saw when you broke in.

R: I saw that death. The institute was abandoned and the courtyard was full of bones and half-eaten bodies.

Tensor N: What did you do then?

R: I went into the dormitories first. I wanted to see if someone might have survived, by some miracle. But there was nothing except broken things and dead bodies.

Tensor N: I want you to describe the scene in detail.

R: I don't remember it well. I wrote it down as I went, because I could not grasp the horror of what I was seeing. The kitchen was on the ground floor, as was the dining area. I looked there first. Everything had been knocked over, there was dirt all over the floor, broken utensils, raw vegetables that were rotting. There was blood too, old and dried. I didn't find anything useful. Then—then I went upstairs.

Tensor N: And what did you find?

R: The bodies.

Tensor N: Go on.

R: I—There were, I think, six—were there six? I think there were six. Their throats had been bitten. A few of them had their bellies slit. It had been days. The smell—

Tensor N: Where were they?

R: All over. The second floor was all bedrooms. I think

they barricaded the stairs with furniture. Something had destroyed it. There was nothing left but shards and splinters. Two Tensors died at the barricade. One got as far as the rooms before they were killed.

Tensor N: How did you know they were Tensors? There were non-Tensorate staff in the institute as well.

R: I . . . assumed, from the way they were dressed. It is possible they were not Tensors. The floor bore scars of slackcraft. Something had burned. But it may not have been the humans.

Tensor N: What do you mean?

R: They were too scared. They died fleeing—why would they flee, if they could fight? I think whatever attacked them manipulated the Slack. The institute was breeding adept animals, weren't they?

Tensor N: I'm the one asking the questions.

R: I read some of the logbooks that I saw.

Tensor N: In the dormitories?

R: No, a different building. I was in the laboratories—

Tensor N: Let's stay in the dormitories. What did you do on the second floor?

R: I . . . walked around. I was trying to understand what happened.

Tensor N: What did you take?

R: Nothing. I took nothing. I found nothing of use. Someone must have gone through their closets before I did; I found only clothes and toiletries. No journals or letters. No, wait, I found some light captures. But I didn't take them.

Tensor N: You think someone took their letters but left the bodies lying there? To rot?

R: I do not know what other explanation there could be. All their other belongings were intact and untouched. Whatever happened, happened fast. They had no time to pack, or hide or put away things. Someone else must have done it.

Tensor N: But it wasn't you.

R: It was not.

Tensor N: It'll go much harder on you if you lie to us, little lady.

R: I am not lying. Nor am I a lady, but I don't expect you to understand.

Tensor N: You're right. I don't understand why you're making things harder on yourself.

R: Why interrogate me, if you will not believe what I say? I am telling you the truth. Do not dismiss me just because it is not what you want to hear.

Tensor N: You're wasting my time. Move on. What happened next?

R: After the dormitories, I went to the laboratory building. I could hear something moving around the buildings, but I didn't see anything. It made me more cautious. Something had broken the door in; it was a big metal door, the height of two floors. I thought the creature might be sleeping in there, but I went inside anyway. Thankfully, the laboratory was unoccupied. Just some tanks and empty cages. Maybe a few dead animals. Some Tensors had definitely died there, but the creature must have dragged the bodies outside. I found books with descriptions of the experiments. That's how I knew they were trying to breed adepts. They were testing the animals for slackcraft abilities. Your Tensorate said the institute was for farm animals—that was a lie. They were trying to make weapons. For war.

Tensor N: War? You're reaching. Farms need to be guarded too.

R: Who needs a naga hybrid to guard rice paddies? These animals were bred for war, and you know it. You can see what they did when they were set free. You saw the massacre. Wild creatures do not kill with such precision, nor with such efficiency.

Tensor N: And you could tell that just from reading the journals? How long were you in there?

R: Not long.

Tensor N: And again, you took nothing with you?

R: You are correct. You must understand, Tensor, that the beast was free in the compound at that time. I had not seen it yet, but I knew I was not alone. I did not dare linger in any one place.

Tensor N: So, where did you go next?

R: The mill where they'd kept the beast.

Tensor N: The mill?

R: The tall, round building. It was behind the laboratories.

Tensor N: Tell me what you saw in there.

R: It wasn't pleasant.

Tensor N: Tell me what you saw.

R: The building is where they kept the beasts, the naga hybrids. Half-naga, half-raptor. There were two of them. One had escaped. The other one . . . It was dead. Several days dead. Have you smelled that particular stench before, Tensor? A dead cat, a dead dog, something?

Tensor N: I've seen my share of bodies.

R: I ask that you imagine this was ten times worse. A hundred. The air was unbreathable.

Tensor N: What did you do?

R: I ran back outside.

Tensor N: Into the courtyard with all the dead bodies?

R: The air there was open.

Tensor N: You didn't enter the main institute building?

R: I did, after visiting the animal pens. I think this will be of little interest to you; there was nothing there. Only bones. What you really want to hear about are the caverns. Am I wrong?

Tensor N: All right. Tell me what you saw in the caverns.

R: Be prepared. It's a long story.

PART TWO

THE FUGITIVE

Chapter Seventeen

[1162.07.22]

Good evening. The sun falls upon an empire stewing in its rot and corruption, upon a Protectorate where well-fed children play in manicured gardens while orphans starve in the gutter, upon mountains full of ugly secrets and cities determined to keep them buried. It sets upon the disgraced former Tensor Chuwan Sariman, an outlaw in word and deed <u>and</u> name. And if this is to be an outlaw's diary, then I should treat it as such.

This is my truth, my record of everything that's about to happen. The heavens know that the Protectorate will tell <u>their</u> version of my story, and it will be nothing but lies coated in horseshit. I can see it already: behold this brat, who benefited from the generosity of Kuanjin society but reverted to the barbarism of her Kebang roots anyway.

Well, fuck you all. You can't control me anymore.

Let's start where we last ended. I'd stolen the transcripts from the late Tensor Ngiau's office. When I decided to keep them, I knew that I would never return to the Ministry of Justice. There was no way my crimes wouldn't come to light, no way I wouldn't get caught if I went back. I had thrown my lot in with the rebels.

I panicked. I panicked a lot. I thought about the life I'd scraped together. The small house I'd managed to buy in the city, where Kayan could always come for shelter. The job that let me feel like I was making a difference. I almost changed my mind.

And then I remembered that I made a difference by helping people. Doing the right thing. What I had on my hands was so much bigger than me, and worrying about my future was not just foolish but also selfish. I thought of Cai Yuan-ning and her anguish.

I got back to work.

Cut off from the resources I needed now that the investigation was over, I had one lead left: Cai Yuan-fang's sister. But it was more than enough for me. I waited for the dark of the first night-cycle, when the dew chills upon the nape of your neck, and stole into the Registry of Births and Deaths. Except that I got lost in the sprawling complex and nearly got caught twice, because I am not nearly as good as I like to tell myself. It was a ridiculous sort of good luck that allowed me to reach my objective in one piece, as though the Slack had obligingly bent itself around reality to serve me. (Which is a stupid thing to think ... or is it?)

In any case, I made it. In a dusty, lightless hall filled with shelves of scrolls, using the barest of slackcraft to work a sunball and praying no one would detect anything, I found the records for Cai Yuanfang's family. One sister, Cai Yuan-ning. The registry told me where she lived.

I knocked on her door in the second night-cycle. When nobody responded, I tried to push her window in, only to be confronted by the muzzle of a black-market gun. She recognized me. I saw fear but also terrible courage. "What do you want, Tensor?"

"I'm not here as a Tensor," I said. "Not anymore." This didn't convince her, so I said, "Would a Tensor try to break into your house this way?"

She conceded. "No, they would have just torn the door down." And so we declared a fragile truce laced with suspicions. It was a start.

Yuan-ning's brother Yuanfang had been her only family; both their parents were dead. It's a story I know too well: a poor family (generations of tanners, although Yuan-ning works as a seamstress now), the son burning the midnight oil until he was good enough to pass the Tensorate Academy's admissions exam. A first for the family. Their bright hope. "I gave up everything for him," she said. She abandoned her own schooling to work so the family could afford expensive private tutors for her brother. "He promised to look after me when I'm old." And now she has nothing: no parents, no brother, no hope.

I showed her the transcript of Rider's interrogation. "This is what they tried to hide from me," I said. "Hideous experiments and secrets protected in the rock under the institute."

She told me, "You don't even know."

From the darkness of her private room she excavated a stack of letters. Yuanfang's letters. She treated them like they were more precious than gold—and I <u>understand</u>. They're all she has left of her brother. I wanted to take the important bits as evidence, and she shot that down like an errant sun. I could <u>read</u> them, that was all. I can only summarize what I read, since I wasn't allowed to keep any of it or even copy down his words, because . . . Fine. I won't speak ill of her.

- Yuanfang worried about things all the time. Other people, small animals, the state of the world, whether his sister was eating enough.
- His letters mentioned names that weren't among the list of the dead. This means that the institute had secret staff nobody knew about. (fucking fantastic)
- Yuanfang was shy and had difficulty getting along

with people. If someone as reclusive as him knew this many unlisted staff, how many more worked in the secret caverns?

- There were definitely caverns under the official institute, run by a separate, unknown branch of Tensors accountable to nobody else.

- Yuanfang had no idea what went on there. None of the Tensors working aboveground were allowed into the caverns. There was a single point of access in the main building, and it was always heavily guarded.

- He had strange, recurring dreams that troubled him more than dreams should. (So, I'm not crazy)

- Once, in the dark half of a night-cycle, he woke to see a child dressed in white standing in the middle of the courtyard. By the time he put clothes on and ran downstairs, the child was gone.

- The next day his supervisor tried to convince him that the child was one of his troubling dreams. Sure, Tensor Xiang. That sounds likely.

- That night, Yuanfang gathered what courage he possessed and slipped into the caverns. He found "strange and unspeakable" things there. And refused to go into any further detail. (What was down there? Human bones? Disgusting orgies? I need to know)

- Crucially, he found a set of large fish ponds that he had seen in one of his recurring dreams. All identical, down to the fish stocked in those murky waters. He nearly lost his mind (understandable).

- This was his last letter to Yuan-ning. As though the fortunes would let slip the truth so easily.

The one thing about these patchwork pictures that truly struck me, like a fist to the gut, was his description of that particular dream. That fucking dream with the fish in the pond and the teacher watching. Because it was <u>my</u> dream. And the fishponds were <u>real</u>. All this time, I've been dreaming of something that exists in the real world—something from those notorious caverns that hangs so frustratingly beyond my grasp! I think I impressed Yuan-ning with the breadth and depth of my filthy vocabulary when I read those parts.

But I don't care. She can judge me. I'm not crazy. Heavens above, I'm not crazy. I wasn't overreacting when I found these strange dreams unsettling. They <u>are</u> connected to this sorry affair, even though I don't understand how.

Something here stinks stronger than a sardine box. Is someone planting these dreams in my head, same as they did in poor dead Cai Yuanfang's? And who could it be?

The next step was clear as blood in a water dish. There's one person I know who has been in those caverns (almost certainly) and is still alive (most likely). Rider, the outlaw. I told Yuan-ning that I was leaving to find the leaders of the Machinist rebellion in the Grand Monastery. Would she join me?

To my surprise, Yuan-ning said yes. And not just that. She said, "You're wanted by the Tensorate now, aren't you? So, you can't just walk through Chengbee to get to the Grand Monastery. You'll get arrested. And if I'm with you, I'll get arrested too. So, we'll have to think of something else." I must say I'm deeply impressed by her and her willingness to trudge through the waist-deep ocean of sewage that is the inner workings of the Protectorate. She may have nothing left to lose but her life, but that still counts for <u>something</u>. Her guts are lined with steel, and I'm glad we got to meet.

Yuan-ning has a friend, Old Choo, who drives a cart and collects night soil from various Protectorate buildings. He's fetching us at first sunrise tomorrow and taking us to the Grand Monastery. Presumably with his nightly cargo still loaded in his cart. That's marvelous—we shall arrive before the rebel outlaws, stinking of old shit.

How fitting.

Chapter Eighteen

Here I am, tucked in the Grand Monastery, a reprobate
and an outlaw at last. It was easier getting in than I expected—I thought we were going to be interrogated.
Tied up. Thrown into cells until they could make sure
we weren't actually spies. But Yuan-ning and I were
welcomed like old friends. Offered food and water and
lodging for no reason other than that we asked. Either
I have forgotten what true generosity feels like, or they
have an agenda.

(Now that I've written it out, that feels uncharitable.
I remember the village I grew up in, where houses were
not barricaded behind white walls and doors were always
open, strangers welcomed into our midst with no questions asked. Hungry? Have some food. Tired? You can
stay for the night. Long way to go? Take these supplies
with you. I miss that. I miss the warmth of my mother's
hearth and the sound of easy laughter from the commu-
nal weaving halls.)

I met the ones in charge here. Quick impressions, all I have time for:

- The Head Abbot, Thennjay Satyaparathnam. I've never met him in person before, but he is just as the stories tell: tall and handsome and full of easy laughter. He was the first to welcome us, and we warmed to him immediately. He has a deeply reassuring manner, and we could use all the reassurance we can get.

- His second-in-command, the once-prophet Sanao Mokoya. The stories they tell about her are so wild, it's hard to know what to believe. But in the flesh? Intense, hard to understand, the kind of person who thinks fifty things and says only three. Her trust is much harder to win, which is frankly smart of her. She's also very pregnant. So much more than I expected, based on the interrogation transcripts. The far north is no balmy pleasure village. I can't believe she was out there just last week.

- Her sibling, Sanao Akeha, the terrorist outlaw. Dangerous, and they know it. The kind of person who they paint as a noble hero in the stories but are really just thugs with the right kind of motivation. A killer with a noble cause is still a killer. They trust me even less than their sister does. Fair enough. I was the one who selected Ngiau Chimin to interrogate them, despite knowing her sadistic tendencies. I deserve all their suspicion. (I need to be mindful of their pronouns—I've been corrected too many times already. Let's try not to give them more reasons to murder me.)

- Then there's Rider, the other outlaw. Hard to read, guarded, but generous with their patience. A gentle exterior, but tough on the inside. Not quite what I expected. I'm not sure I'll ever get used to the way they fold the Slack to move around.

- And finally, there's Yongcheow, Akeha's partner. Don't eat anything he cooks.

Rider kept meticulous records of their journey into the caverns. May the fortunes bless them and keep them forever safe. I told them about what the Tensorate did with the transcript of their interview, and they said, "I thought that might happen. . . ." They were less dismayed than they were unsurprised. After all, living in the Protectorate was much worse for them than it was for me.

They let me copy from their journal, which was recorded on some kind of slackcraft device I'd never seen before, stolen from the Tensorate. I made light-replicas of the journal entries and they're mine now. They're proof that I'm on the right path.

I've found what the Tensorate was trying to hide.

Stolen children and hideous human experiments.

See, Rider had a twin. When the babies were born—sickly, with soft bones—their rich trader parents sold the infants to Quarterlander merchants, but one of them was stolen by Tensors before they could cross the Demons' Ocean. Rider has spent years tracking down their missing twin, only for all the leads to point to that terrible hole in the mountains.

"Why is the Tensorate after twins?" I asked.

"Twins are more likely to be prophets," they said. "And we think that prophets might be able to influence the outcomes of events, given the right circumstances."

I said, "Are you saying that prophets not just see the future, but can also control that future? What about Sanao Mokoya? She's a prophet—can <u>she</u> control the future?

They said no. It's theoretically possible, but she's never managed it.

I thought about my dreams, about the underground ponds, and the fish forced to swim in patterns. Is that what they were doing? Kidnapping twins en masse and goading them into warping the fabric of the world, in hopes that a spark would be kindled into flame in one of them?

They'd only need one, after all.

I asked Yuan-ning if she wanted to read the journal entries, but she said no. She's not yet ready to face what happened in those awful final hours.

I gave Sanao Mokoya and the Head Abbot a list of names that were mentioned in Yuanfang's letters but weren't on the list of the dead. Mokoya recognized one of them immediately. It turns out she has a network of spies (of course) who feed her the names of Tensors involved in suspicious projects. She recognized High Tensor Gu Shimau, the oldest son of her mother's childhood friend. He was previously a Minister of Agriculture until he was pushed out in favor of a younger man. Still, he came around the Tensorate central administration often. He met with ministers, he hosted gatherings in his sprawling mansion, but no one could ever tell me what the fucker did. Mokoya said his personal interest was the transmission of physical traits from parent to child. So, he's the exact sort of person who might conduct bizarre, hidden experiments on children. I remember him—he could never smile properly. It always came out as a leer. A beady-eyed smirk. My skin feels infested by insects just thinking of it.

I . . . may have volunteered to break into his house and unearth all the evidence I could. I was all ready to go in by myself and fight off every obstacle with my fists. I wanted it. I didn't care if it was a bad idea.

Instead, Rider will come with me. They'll take me into

Gu's mansion with their unnerving Slack-folding ability, and I will quietly, <u>unobtrusively</u> steal his records. Hopefully, we will then return to the Grand Monastery, in one piece.

Thank goodness the Head Abbot has a cooler head than I do. Who knew that the life of an outlaw involved so much reason and sense?

Chapter Nineteen

Rider's Writings, Part I

An elaboration on the events covered in the fragment of the interrogation that I have.

———————

I head now across the bleeding plains. The sun seems to rise and fall faster here, and the sky alternates between blinding whiteness and the deepest crushed blue. I call this a plateau, but only because it doesn't climb and climb like a mountain's face. The ground here is neither easy nor flat. It goes up and down; there are ridges that rise above my head, and ditches to break an ankle in. Deep fissures split the grey stone.

Yet life clings to this inhospitable surface; there are yellow bonetrees as tall as I am, and huge spreading succulents the size of houses. Bloodgrass carpets the spongy dirt that sprouts between knuckles of stone. During the sunfall hours, it lights up with pale bioluminescence and all I can see before me are rows of silver filigree, like fingerbones of the dead.

Perhaps the landscape would be less unsettling if it were quiet, but the wind here never ceases, and it has a strangely human quality to it, like a keening widow. In the dark, I sometimes imagine real words in the high, thin sound, and then an unreasonable fear seizes me. It feels like the landscape itself is speaking to me, and it does not want me here.

I am not superstitious, I do not believe in spirits and demons like some do, but this desolate hellscape plays games with your mind. It makes you doubt your senses. Rational thought falls away. The Slack twists in strange ways here, braided in bizarre patterns that cannot be natural but surely could not be man-made. I wonder about the Tensorate laboratory and the experiments they have conducted. Are they responsible for this deformation of the Slack? What have they done to distort it so?

I do not think I am alone on this plain. I do not mean that Tensors or Machinists might be following me. No, there are animals who live in this inhospitable climate: large ones, the size of livestock. If they did not live here, they died here, leaving behind sets of bones wedged into the rocks. Narrow skulls and the knotted cords of spinal columns, desiccated and white, gristle hardened into chalk by the wind and the cold. I can't tell what creatures these were. I am no naturalist, and the fauna of the Full Lands is still unfamiliar to me.

Their empty grey eye sockets tell me nothing. Some have strange knobs like horns, others jaws full of sharp teeth. What killed them? How did their remains come to be left here? And why are there no living examples upon the plain, darting among the rocks, feeding from the bonetrees and the bloodgrass? Mysteries stack upon mysteries, and I have no explanation for any of them.

In any case, I will find proper shelter when I retire for the night. It will take me two days to cross this plain, I think. I cannot walk, and folding the warped Slack is difficult and dangerous. It has become clear to me how ill suited I am to this task. I was prepared for my quest to be a struggle, but it is one thing to imagine difficulties, and another to live through them.

I traveled perhaps another fifty li today. The landscape continues to grow stranger and my head continues to grow heavier. The air here is thinner and my lungs struggle harder than ever to fill. I am not sure why. I have not climbed any higher since yesterday. Everything should be the same, yet it is not. I blame the permanent bend in the Slack here; the laws of the world behave differently. Is the Tensorate in the business of deforming reality? I shudder to think what they might do once they perfect this.

I've finally caught sight of one of the animals whose bones festoon the crevices of this land. It was some sort of buck in war's colors, deep red shot through with black, antlers spread wide over its head like the branches of a dead tree. It was the antlers that made me think it was a deer: I saw it only briefly, and it was very far off. It ran when it caught sight of me across the plain, and only then did I see that it had at least six legs, thin and black and clustered. The way its body moved as it leapt away made it look segmented.

What was it? I cannot say. But I am sure it is not a natural thing; the way it was put together said that the hand of nature had not been involved. If I had to guess, I would say the wretched thing was an escapee from the secret laboratory. We have already seen what Tensors are capable of crafting out of the wreckage of a living thing. A wholly unpleasant thought, being alone on this plain with these twisted creations.

The more I see of the area the more anxious I become, thinking of what I will find at the end of my journey. My mind conjures formless, terrible ideas of what might have been done to my twin. The journal that Junhong found only detailed the early years of their life, when they were still reasonably human and reasonably normal. I dread to think what has been done to them in the decades since. What if all I find is a monster, twisted beyond recognition, physically and mentally scarred from years of being tortured by the Tensorate? What if I am too late?

That's the worst part of it all. What if I could have saved them if I had rescued them earlier? I waited until I was safe in my own happiness before starting to look for them, and all that time, they were alone and chained to this fate.

My greatest fear is not that I will find some sort of half-animal creature, wild-eyed and untamed. It is that I will find a genuine monster: someone perfectly human but with a heart of stone, turned cruel from enduring years of cruelty. What if they are not a tool enslaved by the Protectorate but a willing blade? What if they are proof of what I should have known all along—that there is something broken inside me, only waiting for the right environment to bring it out?

———

I found the strange buck-creature that I saw yesterday. Or what remained of it, at least. It was the body I first came across, lying in a shallow ditch against a tall column of stone, missing its head and a good chunk of its front half. Close up, I could see that it was about the size of a horse, and it had an equine, muscular build as well. It must have been strong when it was alive. Yesterday I guessed that it had six legs, but that number was actually eight, four on each side. The poor thing was a chimera, the body mammalian and coated with a sheen of dark fur, but the limbs like crab legs, jointed and covered in a hard, iridescent shell.

By the time I reached it, the carcass was no longer warm, and the blood had congealed on the ground and on the ragged edges of the flesh, so I guessed it had been dead for a sun-cycle at least. Whatever killed it had left three deep gashes in its side, and if those were claw marks, they must have belonged to a predator around Phoenix's size. Scavengers had gotten inside the body cavity, leaving tiny bites in the flesh and small toothmarks on the ribs. They were hiding on the edge above me, deep in the cracks in the rock. When I looked up, all I saw were the silver coins of their eyes staring at me. They made chirping noises like bilixins, but I do not think they were birds; when I tilted my head to get a better look, I saw flashes of fangs in the dark. For whatever reason, they left me alone. Perhaps they are afraid of humans.

Following the thick trail of blood led me to more of the creature, abandoned at the foot of a bonetree. Just the head and a few red lumps of upper vertebrae, possibly detached when the antlers got caught in the bonetree roots. The creature had two pointed fangs like mousedeer do, strange to see on a horse-sized head. The antlers were beautiful, though, smooth and pearlescent, each one splitting into a dozen branches that swirled and twisted around each other like a fine carving. I could see a head like this cleaned and displayed in a Tensor's vanity cabinet, stuffed full of cotton and given glass eyes. I have no doubt Khimyan would have loved something like this; she would have cut the head off the creature herself.

I tried to lift the head to get a better look, but I thought it blinked—and in fear, I dropped it and folded as far away as I could. Now that I am safe in shelter and can call up memories of the incident with the cushion of hours in between, I am sure it was only a trick of the light, the sun playing over the glassy surface of its corpse eyes. I overreacted.

This place presses on me with all its hostility: the air like a white demon's breath, cold and dry and thin; the alien landscape with its fruitless trees and thick fleshy grass; the unexplainable warping of the Slack that makes it as unpredictable as a wounded tiger. Fear is my constant companion, turning in my chest like a coiled snake, sliding through my limbs and poisoning my veins.

In any case, I have found the Tensorate facility, against all the odds. All this time, we had thought that the laboratories were hidden here because of the caves so that the Tensors could conceal their abhorrent activities in a natural formation. We were wrong. On the horizon I see that the plain has been cleared of brush and flattened. A series of buildings huddles flush against the flanks of the mountain, grey and square, fenced in by a Slack barrier, or the remains of one—it is so weak that I know I shall have no problem getting by it.

The Tensors <u>built</u> their laboratory out here, in this inhospitable place, and I have to wonder why. What was it they wanted to hide so badly they had to go to the ends of the world to do it, to a place where no human could hope to live? There is a strange stillness to the compound that I cannot explain—it seems empty of people. Perhaps the Slack is so distorted here, I can no longer tell. But I have not seen a soul since I last killed those Tensors who came after me. It does not bode well.

I suppose I will find out.

———

Because of the dangers ahead, from now on I will record my observations as often as I can. If I perish here, these will at least be a record of my last hours, in my own words.

———

I am at the gates of the compound. The place is abandoned: as far as I can tell, it is as empty of life as it appears in the Slack. But it is not <u>long</u> abandoned. The buildings are relatively clean, their walls mold-free, the masonry uncracked. The barrier generators that protect the compound have not yet fallen into disrepair, and the barrier has only failed because several generators have been crushed to pieces. An ominous beginning, if I may.

It turns out that the deer-creature had ten legs after all. I found the rest of it, the shoulders and the haunches, in the courtyard of the compound. It had been stripped to the gristle, the dull clay under it still damp with the blood. At least it was in good company. The courtyard was a dumping ground of bones, scattered thick enough to crunch underfoot. Some of them were from ungulates, others smaller creatures. I saw several ribcages that were clearly human. And they weren't old—even the most dried-out specimens still had flesh clinging to the scarred yellow curves, half in the slow process of drying out.

It is clear that something catastrophic has befallen the facility, and hence the reason for its abandonment. Or was it abandoned? It's hard to say. There are a lot of bones here. A lot of fresh bones. This is a lair.

I dread going into the buildings to see what's left. But I must.

I entered the first building to the left. These are living quarters, as far as I can tell, wooden partitions and stairs built within the stone walls. A kitchen with granite fixtures, woks and pots lying abandoned. The larder has been ransacked, and not neatly. I walked through the building to survey the wreckage. Things smashed on the floor, trinkets, blank scrolls. Food trampled and turning to mush. Occasionally, I caught the scent of deeper decay, the sharp punch of rotting meat.

I tried to find the source of this smell, which was a mistake. It led me up the main flight of stairs. I first realized something was wrong when I saw the claw marks along the banisters and on the side of the walls. The smell only grew stronger and more unpleasant as I climbed to the top of the stairs, which were a jungle of splintered wood. Between the ache in my hips and the fear in my chest, I almost turned around, but I knew that I would never solve the mysteries before me if I allowed myself to become timid. So, I went forward.

Four bodies sprawled across the head of the stairs, soft with decay, flesh ruptured, ropes of intestines melting into black mush. I don't know who they were; I could not stare at them for too long, their hollowed faces with discolored, waxy skin. I hurried down the corridor and found two more bodies, probably cut down while fleeing. Long tears down the back, muscles peeling away from the spine. I knew the patterns of those wounds: raptors. Escaped guard animals, perhaps, or worse. I saw burn marks along the corridor, but from what I know of Tensors, they are terrible at slackcrafting under pressure. So, who scorched these? The attackers?

I can only imagine the terror that these hallways have seen. Sometimes, violent deaths leave their mark on the Slack, but the Slack here is so twisted, death makes no difference.

Despite my horror, I still had to examine the upper floor. These were the dormitories, stacked with closets full of clothes and washbowls and handheld mirrors. Things had been scattered across the tops of tables and beds, the way busy people often will. Someone's innerwear was still draped over the back of a chair. Death came too swiftly for them to react.

Strangely enough, I found no personal writing. There were plenty of books: academic scrolls, tawdry novels, copies of the Instructions. But no journals or letters of any sort. Perhaps this is deliberate; maybe they were forbidden from communicating with the outside world or from writing their thoughts down.

In one of the rooms I found a light capture that had gotten caught under the edge of a closet, face down. It showed a group of Tensors in two rows, one seated and one standing, in the courtyard that is now a boneyard. They were smiling in this light capture, these sixteen people; it looked like genuine happiness. They were proud to be here, excited to do important work. I studied the black-and-white lines of their faces and wondered which of them were the corpses collapsing into stringy pulp in the corridors. Or which of them lay scattered in the courtyard in tooth-marked pieces.

There's another presence in the compound. Something big that moves with sibilant noises and sharp clicks. I haven't seen it, but I can hear it, distant but distinct. Sometimes, I can feel it in the Slack, as though glimpsed between wind-teased layers of bedlinen. Once, I thought I heard loud breathing in the courtyard, and ran to the window to look. But there was nothing. Am I just imagining things and inventing a monstrous beast where there is none? But the bones do not lie. The copper smell of raw flesh does not lie. Something else lives here.

I must investigate the other buildings now. I am plagued by a heavy sense that the compound has more unpleasant surprises in store for me. I must stay vigilant.

The building on the far right of the compound is a laboratory. It is a long building, a single story like a factory or a tanning shed, with low partitions between the experiment rooms and a shared roof peaked high overhead. Half of the building is occupied by what looks like a series of trials: obstacle courses, cages, tanks of stagnant water gone cloudy with neglect. There are markings on the floor where large pieces of equipment have clearly been moved away.

In the other half are rooms equipped with buckets and drainage systems, and long metal tables with lips around the rims, still bright and sharp. Metal implements line the walls and cabinets in neat rows. More ghosts of missing machinery. This is where they conducted their experiments on animals.

From the books and charts left behind, I know what they were doing. Mixing animals of the earth and the skies, of the jungles and of the waters, hoping that in their furtive kneading, they could do better than nature. The Tensors would test the abilities of these animals, shocking them with electricity, submerging them in water, testing their heat endurance. Did these poor creatures, pushed to their limits, turn upon their tormentors and wreak the carnage I see here? I could hardly blame them if they did.

Where are the pens for these animals? There must have been dozens of them, yet I do not see a place for them to live. They must have been caged up, at least.

I still have not found any evidence that my twin was ever here. I can only pray that they were not subject to the same tortures as these poor animals.

I write this from the relative safety of the courtyard, having fled from a building next to the laboratory. I could not stand to be in that building a moment longer. I had mistaken it for a grain mill, which left me unprepared for what I would discover inside.

The building was in fact a massive pen. The moment I entered, I stopped breathing from the foulness of what was within. I've lived in the slums of Chengbee. I have seen death, I have lived with it, I have smelt it on the fifth day when the skin starts to blacken and the organ-fat bubbles upward in clumps of curdled white. It is a smell that dives down your throat and threatens to lodge there and never leave. But none of it could compare to the intensity of the stench that assaulted me the moment I pushed those doors apart. It was like a physical blow, one that punched the air out of my lungs and replaced it with a miasma of putrefaction. I nearly swooned; I might have relieved my stomach of its contents. Still, I stepped inside. I wanted to see. I had to know.

The creature was indeed as big as Phoenix. It had been dead long enough that its form had melted under the hand of decay; what remained lay scalloped and mottled, sliding off the bone. Its abdomen had burst, the contents spilled across the ground in black gouts. The jaw had come off the skull, exposing rows of serrated teeth. The arms seemed to be partly winged, with some kind of rotting membrane between fingers as long as I am tall. Was this some sort of hybrid between a raptor and a naga?

I noticed that the carcass hadn't been scavenged. Of course, my first thought was that this was the creature responsible for the carnage outside. But if it had been dead for days, then what killed the buck-thing out on the plain?

The building was large enough to hold two of these creatures. Maybe more. I saw chains hanging from the ceiling, heavy enough to hold up a bridge. And then I could not stay within those walls and breathe in that rot a moment longer.

So, here I am, in the courtyard, surrounded by the chewed bones of the dead, sucking in air and trying to clear my mind. I hate this place. Why did I come here?

———

I found the animal pens at last—they were behind the main building, row after row of long sheds with corrugated tin roofs. Each was split into a dozen pens by high walls, and barred with iron alloy gates. The animals were gone, more or less. Some of them left bones behind. Their pens had been broken into, the bars wrenched from their hinges and thrown upon the ground. The smears of blood on the walls and the grizzled clumps of protein within told the rest of the sorry tale. I counted any pens without remains in them as lucky escapees. Lucky enough to flee and be hunted down later, I presume.

I would have explored further, but I heard something moving along the rows—terrifyingly close, a slithering, clicking noise, and then I was struck by a wall of foul odor. All my courage deserted me and I fled. I fold-jumped, of course, but with the Slack here so warped, I couldn't control it. I was lucky. I could have ended up buried in a wall, but instead I ended up in the courtyard, next to the central building. I stumbled through the double doors and found myself in a high, wide receiving hall, interrupted near the back by a floor-to-ceiling tapestry and a marble counter before it.

It is behind this counter that I am crouched now, trying to coax breath back into my lungs. The building has long, graceful windows covered in painted silkglass that looks so fragile, so terribly breakable. I can see the courtyard through them, and it looks empty.

I am keeping watch. I have not seen the creature yet. I can only hope it has not seen me. But my mind keeps saying it is in here with me.

Chapter Twenty

Rider's Writings, Part II

And here it is: the answer to "what the fuck was in those caverns, anyway?"

————————

I suspect I have discovered why the Tensors built their laboratories on this mountain plateau. After my last entry, I waited until my heartbeat had slowed and my limbs had stopped shaking. The creature that stalks these buildings still had not appeared, and I felt that the danger was over for now. So, I began to explore the building instead.

Behind the tapestry I found a massive set of stairs, wide and deep enough to admit an invading army and their siege engines. They led downward, deep beneath the skin of the mountains. They built their institute over this fissure. There's an entire compound down here, spreading deep and wide like the roots of a tree.

I now find myself in a chamber large enough to swallow

a city. There's a lake here, long and wide enough I can barely see the other end. Light comes from above, but I can't see the source. It has a strangely incandescent quality that tells me it's not daylight. I don't know what it is, but it feels oddly peaceful. After the horrors upstairs, the calm here feels like a gentle river, cool and enveloping. There are no bones here, no smears of death, no smells of despair. If I could, I would remain here indefinitely, resting my weary limbs in the gossamer light and listening to the lake whisper to itself.

But I cannot. There are openings carved into the walls of the chamber here, and I must examine them. If this is where they took my twin, there is hope yet. It seems better down here than it was up there.

The deformation in the Slack is even stronger here in the heart of the mountain. It's not safe for me to travel like I usually do—not when the shape of this place's geography is alien to me, not when the glossy black of the lake's surface hides untold fathoms. It would be far too easy to consign myself to a watery end. I will walk. Slowly.

———————

The first chamber on the left yielded a warren of what seem like Tensors' offices, thoroughly cleaned out. I have found nothing: no equipment, no carelessly discarded logbooks, no signs of whatever life previously occupied these premises. Just a series of neat rooms carved into the rock, floors punctuated by smooth blocks of tables and blameless columns to sit on, walls interrupted by the carved-in ribs of cabinets and shelves.

Everything has been scoured clean, as though with acid, with lime. Did those who worked here have more time to evacuate than those who worked on the surface? I wonder what they wrote on these desks. I wonder what they kept on those multitudes of shelves.

––––––––––

The next chamber over is far larger, high and wide as one of the receiving halls in the Great High Palace. A narrow corridor opens out into a yawning space like an assembly area, studded with pools of fish in a deliberate pattern. Everything down here is lit with sunballs that still function, but not for much longer: the light in them is dying, turning brittle and yellow and flickering. Some have already gone out. The ponds certainly needed constant maintenance: in abandonment, the grey water is foul with dead carp, their white bellies floating, long as one of my arms.

Dozens of rooms branch out from the central chamber. Like the offices, these were also picked clean. If not for the furniture carved out of rock, I would be looking at blank rooms, unreadable and inscrutable. But I've found rooms with chairs clustered in groups, and rooms with a single pair of chairs facing each other. And then there are broad rooms with no chairs but with shelf-gouged walls and floors etched with dust, marking the positions where chests and cabinets must have once stood. Everything in these chambers is shorter, the chairs stooping low. When I tried sitting in one, my knees folded to my chest, and I am not a tall person. These were made for children, my love. They kept children here.

They must have been experimental subjects; I am certain of that much. Buried deep within the remote mountains, masked by the bizarre warping of the Slack, held in the thrall of the Tensorate. Did these children ever see the sun? Did they live and die here, their bones sunk at the bottom of the lake? I cannot tell.

My guess is that this chamber was some sort of academy, a place where the subjects came to learn and play. Learn and play, as though they were leading normal lives. My mind conjures images of happy children, smiling and well fed, walking at leisure between these rooms, exchanging jokes amongst themselves and laughing. The stone walls echo with laughter. Right now, these hollows tower over me, passive and inert, their secrets locked behind their unbreakable silence. If they could speak, what might they tell me?

Wait. I think I hear someth—

No. It is nothing. There is nothing. Just the lapping of water, echoing oddly upon these hewn walls. My mind plays games with itself, scaring me like that.

I must continue.

———————

I have found where they kept their subjects. Sixteen cubbies hidden behind a door in the rock, arranged in two rows, back to back. Each square of chalk-white rock is the same: a narrow bed, a desk, a rack of shelves on one wall, and little else. The cubbies are small enough that there is no space to walk or run or jump inside them. The imprisoned children could only sit at the desk to write, perhaps, or lie down on the bed to read. Were they given books to read?

Each cubby had bars across the front. Of course, if these children were adepts—as I'm sure my twin must have been—the bars could not have held them if they truly wanted to escape. But the barriers to leaving a place are not merely physical: this I know better than anyone.

There are doors set into the bars, each one unlocked. I went into one and lay on the bed's flat surface, letting its hardness press against my bones, trying to imagine the life my twin must have led. Staring up at the pockmarked white ceiling, confined to the tiny bounds of this unhappy world. How long were they kept here? What did they know of the world outside? Have they ever seen the pink and lavender of the falling sun, or the dapple of leaves across a summer's forest path? The fear that has dogged me dissolved in the wave of sorrow as I contemplated the misery their life must have been steeped in. By comparison, I have been unfairly fortunate.

At least I found no bodies in the cages.

————————

There is another chamber beyond these, a great oval with pillars of stone holding up the roof, ringed by staircases connecting several floors of recessed cubbyholes. In the center, on the ground floor, a series of laboratory tables, like the ones Khimyan had. I do not know for sure if it was the children who were being experimented on here. As before, those who worked here left nothing behind. But the examination tables are small—they will not fit a child older than ten or twelve—and arranged in pairs.

I have examined the tiers of cubbies above the observation area. And what I found there, I cannot explain. I am not even sure what it is I stumbled upon. There were dozens and dozens of machines welded to the stone, oblong boxes of metal with glass lids. These were slackcraft-operated; I could feel the residual charge in them. But I could not activate the devices or fathom what they were used for. They were meant to hold human beings, but for what purpose? And for how long?

Then I noticed that, like the examination tables, many of these machines were in pairs. Not all of them, but in sufficient numbers for it to be strange. Upon closer examination, I saw that the boxes were labeled, a series of characters and numbers on each. The ones in pairs were labeled in pairs: upper and lower. These boxes held twins. They conducted experiments on twins.

And then I was overcome by exhaustion from having to climb so many flights of stairs, so I sat down to write. I have been steeped in troubled thought, trying to justify why whoever kidnapped my twin from the Quarterlander vessel only took one infant. Why did they leave me behind? Was it the weather that stopped them? Was it their orders? Or did they just decide to leave one child for the Quarterlanders, in hopes that the theft would not be reported?

How cruel are the fortunes! A different knot in their tangled strings and I could have been the one imprisoned here in this house of stone, subject to the whims of those who do not see me as human. But it was my twin who was taken, while I went free.

I know what Mokoya would say at this juncture: "Cruel as the fates might be, they cannot match the cruelty of humans." And she would be right.

She would probably also ask why I still linger in this place, when it is clear it has been abandoned, when it is clear that I will never find what I came looking for. Why do I stay in this hellpit full of death, patrolled by a dangerous, ravenous beast? Because I am not satisfied. I will not leave until I find something of my twin to take back with me. There must be some trace of their existence here. They cannot have vanished without leaving something behind. I want to find it. I want to excavate it from these forsaken walls.

I've found the crypt. The chamber full of the bones of the children who perished here. A long corridor drilled through the rock, honeycombed on either side with alcoves for the dead. Many of the children were buried in pairs, but perhaps a third of the alcoves contain a single skeleton. A lot of them died young, their skulls still soft and their wrists narrow.

Even the air here is muted. I walked back and forth, looking at the rows and rows of remains, trying to guess if any of them might have belonged to my twin. I wonder how Mokoya feels. If Akeha had died in a disaster far from her, would she be able to pick their bones out of a pile of the dead? Would the Slack point her in the right direction, telling her, there, that is the one who lay by your side as you were slowly put together in the womb?

I felt nothing, and I do not know if it is because my twin is still alive, or because I don't know what they would feel like, in life or in death. I never knew them.

Wait. I hear something. What

―――――――――

Mokoya, if you are reading this—if this gets to you somehow—I am sorry. The creature found me. It followed me down the steps.

Now I know what they look like when alive. I was right, I guessed right: they crossed a raptor and a naga. Raptor-shaped but with elongated, membranous arms. The carcass upstairs must have belonged to a juvenile; this one is far larger. And <u>fast</u>. It can turn invisible. One moment it was a sharp white thing standing alone on the shores of the lake, and the next it was gone. I thought at first it had folded away—but then I heard its feet. It was charging toward me. I ducked into the closest opening I could find—it was the row of cells—and barricaded myself in one of the cubbies.

I have escaped the creature's jaws for now, but for how long? I hear the hollow sounds of the beast running itself into the door barring this corridor. Eventually, it will fail. That thing knows I am in here, and it won't let me escape. I am trapped. Even if I could escape this room and find my way to the stairs up, it would be hopeless. I cannot outrun this creature. Already my bones are aflame with exhaustion. It would be faster and simpler to seek death in the clutch of its jaws.

My mind conjures light captures of the last terrifying hours here, the creature breaking loose from its torments, its keepers struggling to restrain it as the others flee. What happened to the children? The Tensors working down here clearly knew they had time to evacuate properly. Somehow, they knew what was about to happen. I can only hope that my twin, if they were even here, was spared all of this horror.

I hear something breaking. It is almost here.

Chapter Twenty-one

That could have gone a lot worse. But it could also have gone a lot better.

We launched our grand break-in during the second sun-cycle. Mokoya's network whispered to her of a clandestine meeting between Gu and Minister Sonami at that time, so we knew he wouldn't be in. Rider took me to his mansion in the White Quarter, skipping across Chengbee in jumps through places they were familiar with—a secluded park here, the upper floor of an inn there. Bless the fortunes, they had been inside Gu's mansion several times before, so instead of folding us into one of his oversized fishponds (what is it with wealthy Tensors and making their houses look like water farms?) or an open furnace, we landed safely in Gu's office. A locked room, full of expensive hardwood furniture, every surface stacked with scrolls and books. We swept up everything that bore the insignia of the Rewar Teng institute, filling two unused chests we found.

Rider was nervous through it all, constantly checking that no one was coming to clean this spotless, obsessively tidied, locked room. Or to investigate the soft noises of chests being shifted across the floor. We were there barely ten minutes before they said, "We have what we want. We should go."

I didn't want to. My gut burned with the feeling that we had missed something, and my gut has never led me wrong. I was staring hard at one particular bookshelf—I don't know what it was, but I wanted to inspect it more closely. It looked perfectly ordinary, and the journals lining its shelves proclaimed themselves to be annual reports of the Tensorate Society of Demographic Studies. But the longer I stared at it, the more convinced I became that it was hiding something.

But just as I was about to touch it, we heard voices, and Rider yanked us, boxes and all, out of the room.

I was furious to find myself on the roof of an abandoned building. I was just on the verge of a breakthrough. I was about to discover something important and they stopped me. I shouted at them. In hindsight: ill conceived. But my blood was boiling, and the stress of the past few days put stupid thoughts in my head and stupid words in my mouth. I accused them of being a coward. I asked if they were trying to sabotage my investigation.

I don't quite remember what they said over the rushing anger in my head, but I think it was something like "<u>Your</u> investigation? It's not <u>your</u> sibling who's missing."

We returned to the Grand Monastery in a thick fog of silence. There were a few raised eyebrows, but nobody bothered to ask what had happened (or none dared to). Instead, all attention was on the treasures we had stolen.

The spoils of our adventure burst with monthly reports from the secret laboratory that ran beneath the institute. In those thin scrolls, written in an impeccable hand (same hand: a single report-writer?), were details of everything we wanted to know. Experiments, materials, and results.

I would very much have liked to look through these documents myself. But Rider had other ideas, pointedly cutting me out of all the discussions. They took charge of what we'd brought back, and only allowed other Machinists to touch them. I got the hint after my questions were pointedly ignored for the second or third time. I'm used to this. Truly. It's the same shit that weak-willed Tensors used to pull on me. Why did I think these people would be any more welcoming of an outsider?

Thus, a secondhand summary of what they found from reading the documents:

- The institute kept a stable of more than sixty children,

unethically sourced from all over the Protectorate.

- Most of them were pairs of twins, but a significant chunk were children who were half of a pair.
- No names. Why bother, when you could just assign them numbers?
- They were between three and ten years of age, thereabouts. Unless I understood it wrongly, they were kept in some kind of frozen state and thawed in batches to be experimented on.
- Guess we now know what they used those rows and rows of pods for.
- We were right. The bastards were trying to breed, or train, someone who could change the course of the future on command.

So. We now know what happened in those caverns, from day to day. But it does nothing for the questions I came here to answer:

<u>What</u> happened on the day the beast escaped? Are these children still alive? Where are they now? How did they get out when the other Tensors didn't?

Did the children foresee what was about to happen and have their minders evacuate them early?

Did they <u>cause</u> the disaster?

When I am finally judged at the gates of Hell, I will tell them that I tried my best to reconcile with Rider, and it's not my fault it didn't happen. I carefully asked if they recognized any of the children in the journals. Maybe one of them would be their twin?

They said, "How could I know someone I have spent no time with from a handful of sentences written by someone who does not see them as human?"

Fair answer, but I can tell when I'm being scolded. I'm not an idiot.

Later, Cai Yuan-ning came by with a bottle of rice wine and sat by me while I contemplated the night-cycle moon. She asked what happened between Rider and me. I told her. I shrugged. "They're right," I said. "Who am I to intrude? I have no stake in this investigation."

She looked strangely at me. "You're joking, right?"

I shrugged again. I'd thrown away the life I'd known to pursue this investigation, only to be told that I had no business being here.

"They're wrong," Yuan-ning said. "After the release of the official Tensorate report, I lost all hope. I thought Yuanfang was doomed never to have justice. But then you showed up. A Tensor, trying to help. I would never have expected it."

We drank the wine. "Now we are blood sisters," she said.

I sit here writing in the waning moonlight, belly warmed with wine and mind slowed with its thick heat.

Soon, the sun will rise for the second night-cycle. And then it will set again, and then it will rise again, and then it will be a new day, and time will go on. And still the mystery of Rewar Teng remains unsolved. Out there is a child with Rider's face and peculiar health condition, hidden away in the dark like a dirty secret. I wonder what they're thinking. I wonder what they're feeling.

I wonder if we'll ever get to meet.

Chapter Twenty-two

How long can a person go without proper sleep before they shatter into a husk of murderous animal emotion? Three days? Two weeks? How much shorter if those sleepless nights are speared through with gravesent nightmares? I feel like death, and I can't tell if it's because my head is infested with ghosts, or if it's because my body is breaking down.

Yes, another night, another fucking fever dream. This investigation will never let me rest.

This dream was vivid. Different. I was a child, stumbling through a strange house that I was supposed to call a home. This alien edifice of hardwood and stone, smelling of unknown perfumes, the marble flooring cold against my feet. In the dark, the hulking shapes of furniture and statuary took on a sinister cast. I was terrified, but I did not want to go back to my new room and lie alone and still with my thoughts. I missed the bare dirt and attap roofs of the houses I was used to.

Their airy interiors filled with laughter. Fear and longing filled me like seawater.

I guess I was looking for something. I don't remember. I stumbled into one of the reading rooms, drawn to it by some unknown force. Its darkness was interrupted by a box, brightly lit from above by an unseen source. The cabinet that contained the puppet. I remember it: a carved and painted rendition of one of the old Kuanjin gods. My father had it commissioned from a master craftsman in Chengbee. I hated that thing, its bloodred face and fathomless eyes and uncannily detailed robes.

It lifted its head and looked at me. It said my name: Sariman. The name given by the ones who birthed me, not the ones who stole me. I walked over, powered by the burning need to know what it had to say. My curiosity has always been stronger than my dread.

I looked into its hollow eyes. It was bigger and heavier than I remember, and its long black beard was missing. Without that goatish feature, the puppet looked much younger, like an egg-faced child.

"Sariman," it said. "Sariman, you were right."

"What about?" I asked.

"What your instincts were telling you. And you know how you can find me." It gestured to the room outside its box. "You know this place."

"My parents' home?"

"No. Look closer."

And then I realized that I was not in my parents' house but in another place I'd been before. The Gardens of Tranquility: the cloistered, verdant compound where the Minister of Justice worked and lived. This was Sanao Sonami's home.

I woke with sweat clinging to my skin and anxiety clinging to my mind. It was still dark, not yet a new day. I couldn't sleep, and pain refused to leave my gut and my chest. I went outside and found one of the Grand Monastery's quiet gardens, except that Rider was in it, contemplating the last moon of the day.

I approached them cautiously. I regretted our earlier dust-up, which my anxiety told me was foolish and petty, but the air between us still held a fathomless chill.

They didn't say anything to me, so I asked them, "How deeply do you think Sanao Sonami was involved with all this?"

They looked startled, like I had slapped them. "Sonami? Why would she be involved?"

"She tried to suppress my investigation. That's why I broke from the Tensorate."

Rider looked troubled and stayed quiet for several uncomfortable heartbeats. "I don't know Sonami's reasons for doing things," they said finally. "But she has supported the Machinist movement since its inception.

Whatever her intentions were with your investigation, there must be bigger things at play."

I was so stung by this patronizing dismissal, I nearly blurted, "What could be bigger than finding your twin?" It was only good sense and my survival instincts that kept my mouth shut.

Silence tightened its grip over us. Rider looked so tired. Discouraged. Like the world had finally worn them to the bone. As I scrambled for something to say that wouldn't offend them, they told me, "I'd like to have a quiet moment alone, if you please."

I realized I'd interrupted them in the middle of something private. Keenly aware of the fragility of our relations, I turned and left.

As I reached the boundaries of earshot, I heard them whispering to themselves, "I will find you. I won't give up."

In hindsight, I should have told the truth. I should have confessed why I suspected Sonami knew where the missing children were. I should have told Rider about my dream, about the puppet in my adoptive parents' house, telling me secrets. But I was a coward. I didn't want them judging me, thinking of me as an unhinged country bumpkin.

So, I said nothing. I left them to whatever personal anguish they were wallowing in. I felt guilt as I walked away.

But I was too chickenshit to do the right thing.

It's been some time since then, but instead of fading away like normal, the sense of the dream has been growing inside me. It's no longer just in my head. It's in my heart, in my chest, in my limbs, like a spreading fire. It's telling me I have to do something.

I have to do something.

———————

Well. I did do something.

I went back to Gu Shimau's house. I was going to go it alone, brave the night guards and the high possibility of being caught. I wrote a letter to Kayan just in case I died. I fully believed I was going to the grave. But the dream wouldn't let me rest.

I was sneaking out of the Grand Monastery when Yuan-ning tapped me on the shoulder. Somehow, she was awake, and somehow, she had cottoned on to what I was doing. She said she'd woken to a bone-deep discomfort.

I told her what I planned. "Let me go with you," she said. "This is our blood-sister connection. I knew you were getting into trouble." Which is total bullshit, superstitious nonsense, but I let her follow me down the mountain anyway.

When we got to the city, she stopped one of the night-soil carts and asked the driver where we could find Old Choo. The driver was a friend of the old man's and told us which house he might be at. Thank the fortunes, it was close by, and we found him quickly. So, here I am, scribbling these notes in a terrible jerky hand while breathing in the smell of the cart's fresh cargo. Old Choo will take us to my destination, and I'm going to break in—alone. I'm not putting these people in any more trouble. They can keep watch while I return to that room and find what the hell it is we missed.

Yuan-ning is explaining that her brother helped Old Choo's grandson when he took a bad fall but the family couldn't afford a doctor's fees. See, generosity will buy you more than a lifetime's worth of gratitude. I've told Yuan-ning that if she survives and I don't, nothing else matters except getting this book, with all its writings and letters and documents, into Kayan's hands. I'm sure she can manage.

I think we're here—

———

I was <u>right</u>. I am vindicated, again.

I managed to get into Gu Shimau's office. The mansion was crawling with guards, and not just the usual sellswords and ready louts. Tensors, by the look of it, and defected pugilists. Did he figure out what we'd taken? Or maybe he was just paranoid. Thank the fortunes for their blessings, which I do not deserve, because convenient distractions—small sounds, a bird taking flight, a stone in the shoe—distracted the guards at the right moments. I survived the journey to the office undetected.

I went back to the shelf that had drawn my attention. Pulled out every deadweight journal, one by one. Behind one particularly fat tome I discovered a hidden mechanism. When I pulled the lever, it revealed a hidden compartment. Buried in the wall was a single, narrow shelf, and on that shelf were boxes, and in those boxes was all the damning evidence I need. Private correspondence between Gu and the minister.

This was it. This was what the dream-puppet wanted me to see.

Sanao Sonami was in this from the beginning. She was the one who _directed_ what was going on in that secret laboratory. Gu Shimau might have run the day-to-day operations, but she was the one he answered to. She knew everything.

There was too much to read it all. In hindsight, I should have nabbed the whole damn box for evidence, but I didn't. I just took one particularly relevant letter.

There's one mystery I can solve. I know where one of the children is.

———————

My dear Sonami:

I am so pleased to hear the child is settling down in your place. Treat her well and keep her away from sunlight, and she should give you no problems. Or fewer problems, at any rate. Anyway, you're the expert; who am I to give you advice on child-minding? You raised those two brats, didn't you?

You'll be glad to hear that I've found a buyer for the last sixteen subjects. They'll fetch a fair good price, but I know you don't care about money. Well, there's that. The last sentence in a book thirty years in the writing. It might be crass to say the experiment succeeded beyond our mad hopes, given what happened at the institute, but we got what we wanted. If the cost has to be a few dozen ordinary lives ... Well. No one changes history without sacrifice.

I'm sure you have grand plans for your new pet. Don't forget all the things I've done for you.

Gu

Chapter Twenty-three

So, this is how it ends. Alone, in the dirt, full of graceless revelations and unanswered questions. Death spirals through my veins; already my legs are pewter-weight and I can barely hold anything. Soon, the poison will claim my heart and it will all be over.

After I escaped Gu Shimau's place, I decided to go straight to the Gardens of Tranquility. I knew now that the dream I had was a message. There was no logic to it, just a sense of truth in my heart. And it had not yet led me astray. I knew deeply and intimately that I was being led to the Gardens by someone I couldn't see. Whoever was trapped there—this child who Sonami had taken custody of—wanted me to come to them.

I met resistance in the form of Yuan-ning's practicality. She suggested we go back to the Grand Monastery instead and tell them what we found—but I wanted to barrel ahead. I always want to barrel ahead. This served me well in my career, and now it has been my downfall. I wanted to return to the Grand Monastery with my prize in hand, to show all of them they had been wrong. What an idiotic notion that was. I should have listened to Yuan-ning.

In any case, I did not, so Old Choo drove us to the Gardens. I told the two of them, Yuan-ning and Old Choo, to give me an hour. Somehow, I knew it would be dangerous to get them any more involved. We arranged to meet in the copse of trees in the far west of the Gardens, close by the pig's trail where the night soil carts leave.

I got into the mansion without incident. I knew I would. I'd already understood what was going on, see. These piles upon piles of coincidence, it wasn't the fortunes blessing me. It was the doing of this child. That's why Gu said they succeeded. That's why Sanao Sonami sequestered them in the depths of her home like a pearl. They had what they wanted: made a prophet who could influence the shape of the world. And now I planned to steal this precious thing away.

I let their influence guide me, slipping through small gaps in the Gardens' security, this way and that in the labyrinthine complex. I had only been inside the Gardens once before, but who needs familiarity when you are being led by a prophet? I would creep down the perfumed corridors, passing by carved arches and decorative wood lattices, until I reached a point where I had to decide which way to go. And I would just <u>know</u>. I've often wondered what it's like being one of those fish or birds that travel thousands of li to the place of their birth while not knowing roads or directions or the names of places. At least I die with that question answered.

Just by the Gardens' sprawling library was a set of stairs leading to the basements. I knew with dream-certainty that this led to my destination. I climbed downward for fucking ever, plunging into a damp gloom that strained the eyes and clung to the skin. The walls changed from wood to mortar slurry to raw stone. I was in the bedrock underneath the mansion. I must have descended a hundred yields, maybe more.

By the time I reached the bottom, I was dazed, almost numb, as if the air above had the weight of water and was crushing the ability to think out of me. In front of me lay a web of red string, impressively knotted like a gift box. All good sense had left me by then, so I unthinkingly grasped the central knot, as if I could undo it with my hands. Pain shot up both arms the moment I touched it, and in hindsight I wonder if it was just the poison darts or also a warning from my benefactor. At the merest touch of slackcraft, the ropes undid themselves, reeling back into hidden places in the walls. But by then, it was too late. I was already doomed, even if I didn't realize it then.

I traveled a long dark corridor of stone, its ceiling high

over my head. At the end of it: a massive stone door that had to be pushed in with slackcraft. Behind that? Caves. I don't know how old they were, whether they were carved by hand or slackcraft or machinery—I'm no geologist, I can't fucking tell. But now the chamber was filled with light from massive sunballs strung between its hewn pillars.

In the middle of it all, on a tall flat slab of rock like a dais, sat the one who had brought me here. Up until that point, I wasn't sure what I would find at the end of this gravesent journey. None of the writings around this child prophet had described them. They had barely treated them as human. And after all the horrors I'd read about, I was expecting something monstrous, deformed by cruelty.

But what I found was a child. A child who looked normal, a child who breathed and had blood running in their veins like any other human. Blood that showed as a blush on papery skin that had never seen the sun. That child looked at me with an expression equal parts sadness and longing.

"It's you," I said. Their identity was unmistakable. I was staring into Rider's face, as it might have been when they were ten years old. "You did it. You made the future."

The child shook their head. "No, I didn't. It never works perfectly."

"But I'm here," I said.

"You're not them," they said.

I realized that they had been waiting for their twin. I thought about the argument I'd had with Rider before coming here. Was I meant to have brought them with me? Was this my fault?

"It's hard to control the flow of events," they explained. "It's like directing a drop of water rolling down the back of your hand."

"Water follows the most likely pathway," I said. "But there are many pathways."

They nodded.

I had so many questions, but one burned the brightest of all. "Tell me what happened at Rewar Teng. What did you do?"

"I tried to escape." They looked pensive. "And I <u>almost</u> got away, but I didn't do it right. It's so hard, you know. There's so much more I have to learn."

They had let the beast out, but it wasn't by popping a latch. Nothing so crude. It was the little things they changed: a weakness in the chains, a distracting quarrel between colleagues. Shifting the shape of events so that it became not just likely but <u>inevitable</u> that something would happen. A skill honed over the years, yet still horribly imprecise.

And they were foiled. All their talents aside, they were

still an experimental subject, and their every movement was monitored. The Tensors in charge had instruments to measure small distortions in the Slack. Their plans were detected, anticipated, and the children moved a day before the calamitous events were to take place.

I don't blame the child for the deaths at the institute. They don't understand the impact of what they did. How can they understand the cost of death when they've never experienced enough of life to understand its value?

But the ones in charge. Those gravefuckers. They let the disaster happen. They <u>knew</u> how many would die—and let them. Because they wanted to see if their experiment <u>worked</u>. Those stone-hearted turtle bastards. Those monsters. Someone has to track them down, bring them to justice. It won't be me. It can't.

There was so much more to be said. But standing in that great, cold hall with its artificial light, I had one goal and one goal only: to get the child out of there. I could not bear to see them in this gravesent mockery of safety and shelter, separated from all those who could care for them. I saw a reflection of the little girl I had been, frightened and angry in an alien place, and remembered how that little girl burned with desperation, wishing for the skies to open and for someone to swoop down and rescue her from that place she hated. I wanted nothing more than to save this poor child.

"Come with me," I said. "I know where your twin is. I can take you to them."

But they only looked sadder. "I cannot," they said. "There's slackcraft in my blood that will wake the moment I leave this chamber. Sonami will know what happened. She'll find us before we get away."

If only I had brought Rider with me. They could have folded us off to safety. We could have gotten away, all of us. But it's useless to wish for things to be different now.

The child had a letter for their twin. "Give it to them," they said. "So they'll know the truth."

It seemed so inadequate in the face of what I wanted to do. So underwhelming. A letter? I wanted to deliver freedom. I wanted to enact justice. I heaped foolish and hasty promises on the child. I was going right back to their twin. We were going to come for them immediately. I was going to save them. Soon, they would be free.

I was leaving. They told me, "You touched that red string, didn't you? It's poisoned. Look for the antidote in the chemist's room. It's on the second shelf in the white cabinet, in a small brown bottle shaped like a gourd. You must take it all, or you will die."

And I meant to. Believe me, I meant to. I rushed back upward, through the tunnels of stone and the endless steps, fully intending to find the chemist's room as the child instructed. But urgency burned in my veins like fire, and fear snapped at my heels. The moment I got to ground level, I saw the shadow of a person—a servant? a guard?—vanishing around the corner before me. I was almost caught. Panic took hold of me. No matter what, I knew I <u>had</u> to get out. So I thought, like an enormous fool: Fuck it. I don't feel unwell, I've got time. I can make it to the Grand Monastery. Thennjay's a doctor. We can fix this. See, I thought the poison was slow-acting. And I <u>had</u> to get out. That was the most important thing. So I ran. I headed straight for the outside, where our meeting point waited.

By the time I'd reached the outer Gardens, my heart had started to slow. And by the time I'd reached the pig's trail, my legs were failing me. I knew I'd made a mistake, but by then, it was too late. I collapsed to the ground, and that was that. I won't be getting up again.

How ironic. In my investigation, I ran up against the worst of human malice, but in the end, it was my own carelessness that got me killed. Here I am, lying helpless, waiting for death to claim me. Yuan-ning and Old Choo won't reach me in time. The soil is cold, but I see the sunrise coloring the sky above me, and it's beautiful. I wish Kayan were here. I want to hear that laugh of hers one more time. She would be furious about how foolish I've been, but she knew she was throwing her lot in with a fool when she first kissed me. And she would find it darkly funny that after a lifetime of walking the straight and narrow, this is how I'm going out: a rebel.

Of course, I was still doing the bidding of another, even if I didn't know it. But I own this destiny. I own my death. The child didn't determine everything. At the very end of my life, I am sure of that. It was I who chose to do something. It was I who chose to turn against greed and evil. It was I who chose freedom and truth.

It's all right. It's all right. I know I made the right choices. I found out what I wanted. I found out

Chapter Twenty-four

MESSAGE FROM RIDER'S TWIN

My beloved twin:

It's strange writing a letter to someone you have never met, who is nevertheless the most important person in your life. You do not know me, and I do not know you, but I have spent most of my waking days wondering what you might be like. The Tensors discourage us from learning about the outside. But the Slack brings us dreams that they can't censor. I've seen you sometimes, or I think it's you. You're a lot older than I am. They don't let us grow up here. I wonder what you have seen in this world. I know you're looking for me. That's why I decided I wanted to leave.

I have so many things I want to say in this letter. So many things I want to tell you about my half-life, submerged in sleep most of the time, confined to pens and never left alone. But these are things I want to tell you when I see you in person.

The Tensors are trying to teach us to control the dreams, but they can't control us, no matter how much they try. I'm getting better at shaping the world to my whims. I'm not perfect yet. That's how I got caught. But they can't hold me here forever.

Sonami is treating me well. She has plans for things I don't understand yet, things that spread across the breadth of the land and concern the fate of the Protectorate. But you should get out of the capital as soon as possible. You and all of your friends are in danger.

She gave me a name, but I don't like it. In the long years under the stone, I chose a name for myself: Tau. It sounds nice to me, although I don't know why. I'd like to use it when we meet.

I hope we get to meet soon. I'm going to keep trying. And I'm sorry for all the trouble I've caused. Thank you for not giving up on me.

Your twin,
Tau

Acknowledgments

My deepest thanks to my editor Carl and my agent DongWon for their infinite patience as I repeatedly ripped up this novella and tried to put it back together again. To the Tor.com publishing team—Irene, Christine, Katharine, Mordicai, and Ruoxi— for all their hard work in turning this book into a real thing. And to my friends, who held me together even as I was ready to come apart at the seams.

About the Author

Author photograph © Nicholas Lee

JY YANG is the author of *The Black Tides of Heaven* and *The Red Threads of Fortune*. They are also a lapsed journalist, a former practicing scientist, and a master of hermitry. A queer, non-binary, postcolonial intersectional feminist, they have over two dozen pieces of short fiction published. They live in Singapore, where they work as a science communicator, and have a MA in creative writing from the University of East Anglia. Find out more about them and their work at jyyang.com.

TOR·COM

Science fiction. Fantasy. The universe.

And related subjects.

*

More than just a publisher's website, *Tor.com*
is a venue for **original fiction, comics,** and
discussion of the entire field of SF and fantasy,
in all media and from all sources. Visit our site
today—and join the conversation yourself.